04598608

A MESSAGE FROM CHICKEN HOUSE

In this thrilling wartime novel, a family lives in a lighthouse on the English coast, surrounded by the threat of invasion. Hidden truths, twists and revelations kept me gripped and guessing all the way through – but eventually our heroes have to face up to what *seems* like an impossible choice: family or country? (Which would you choose?) But there's more. Mystical forces are at work, guiding their destinies . . . This is a world of fate, family, myth and adventure – are you brave enough to enter?

BARRY CUNNINGHAM
Publisher
Chicken House

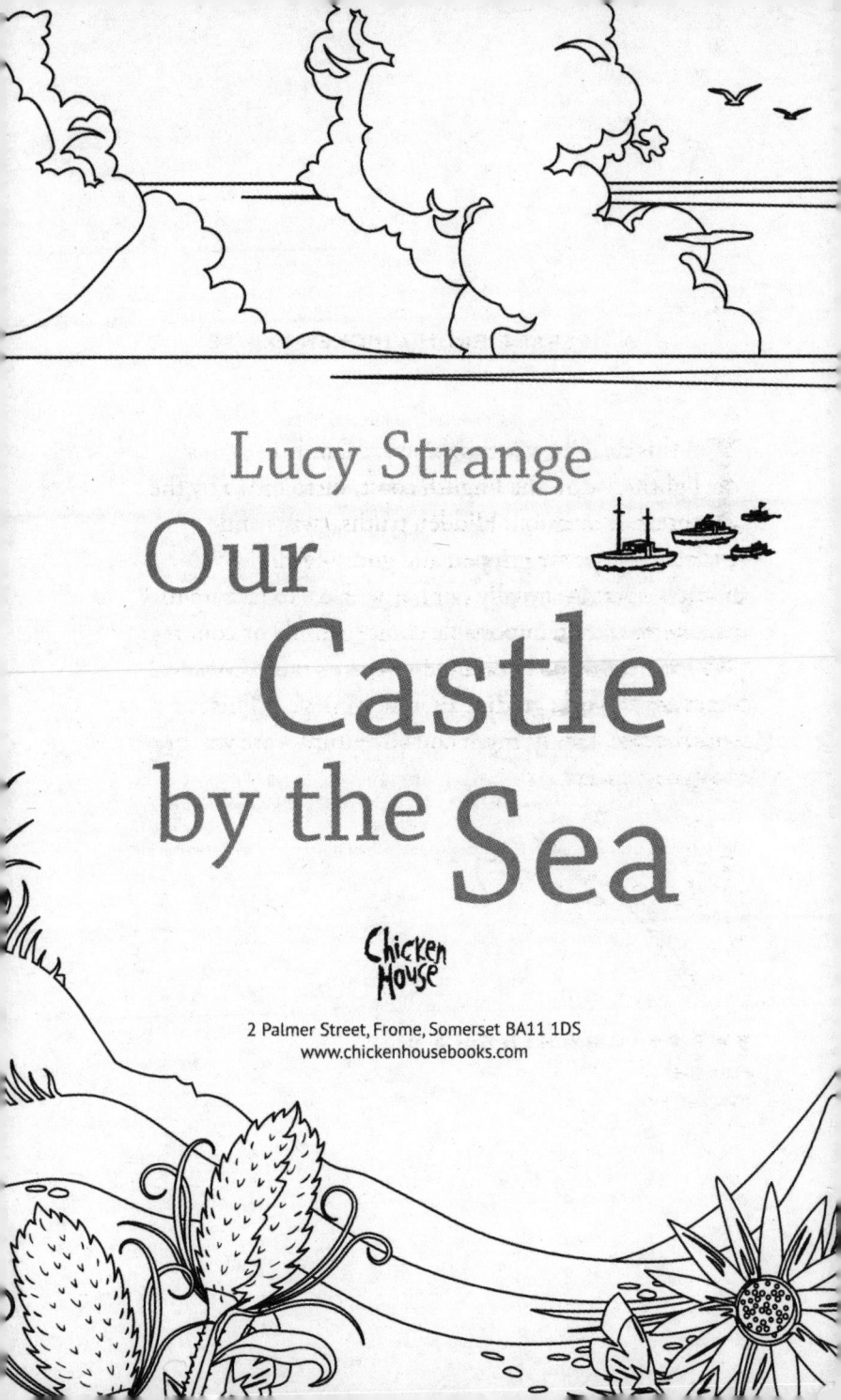

Lucy Strange

Our Castle by the Sea

Chicken House

2 Palmer Street, Frome, Somerset BA11 1DS
www.chickenhousebooks.com

Text © Lucy Strange 2019

First published in Great Britain in 2019
Chicken House
2 Palmer Street
Frome, Somerset BA11 1DS
United Kingdom
www.chickenhousebooks.com

Cover and interior design by Helen Crawford-White
Typeset by Dorchester Typesetting Group Ltd
Printed and bound in Great Britain by CPI Group (UK) Ltd, Croydon CR0 4YY

The paper used in this Chicken House book is made from wood grown in sustainable forests.

3 5 7 9 10 8 6 4

British Library Cataloguing in Publication data available.

PB ISBN 978-1-911077-83-1
eISBN 978-1-911490-52-4

For our path in life ... is stony and rugged now, and it rests with us to smooth it. We must fight our way onward. We must be brave.

Charles Dickens, *David Copperfield*

For James
and for Freddie — our little miracle

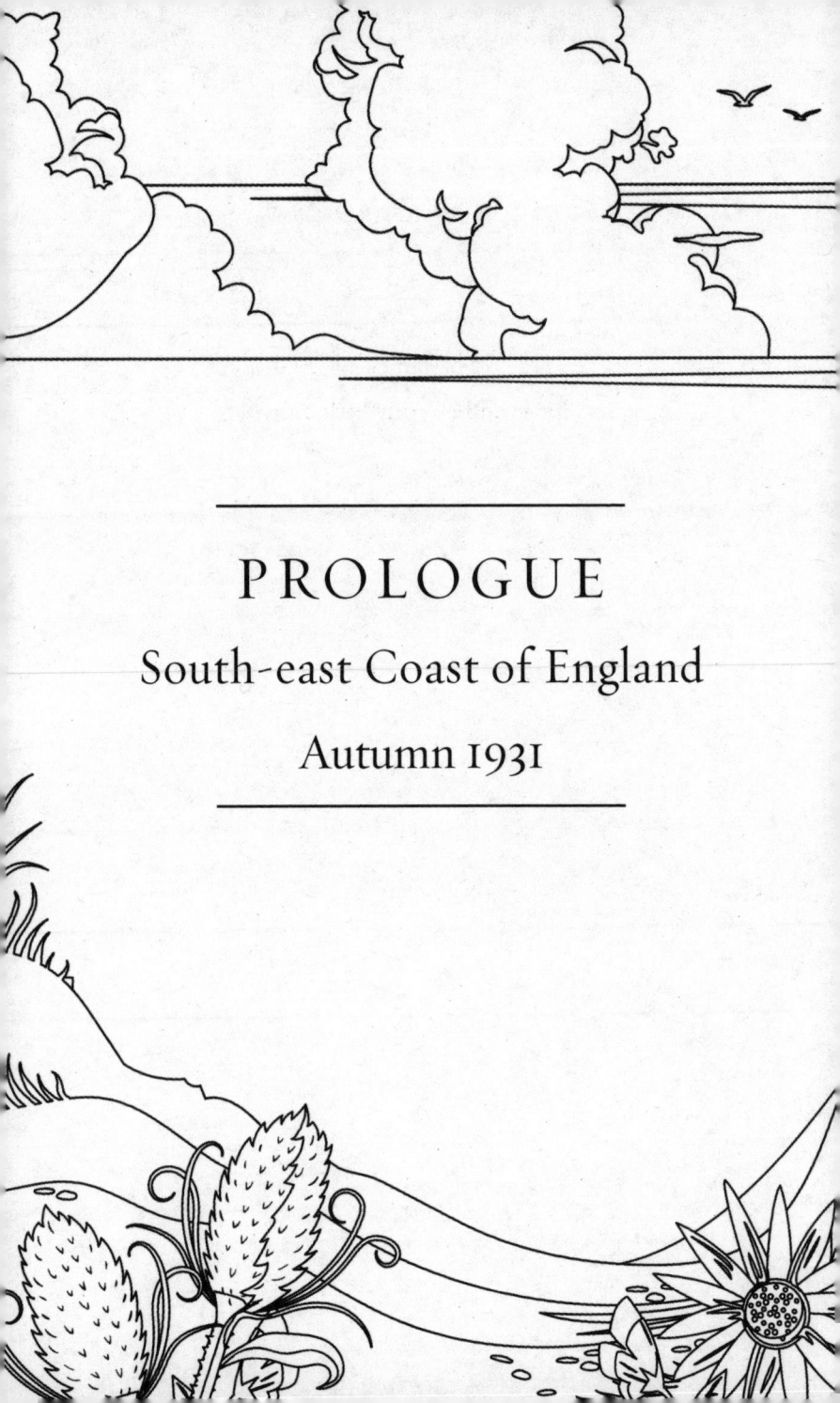

PROLOGUE

South-east Coast of England

Autumn 1931

I was very small indeed when Pa first told us the legend of the Wyrm and the Stones. It was Hallowe'en and he took us out to the standing stones on the clifftop to play snapdragon and tell ghost stories. This was my big sister Magda's idea, and we were almost out of our minds with excitement when Pa agreed. I carried the bowl of brandy-soaked raisins very carefully from the cottage, while Pa lit the way ahead with a lantern. Mags galloped giddily behind, drunk on the night air and fizzing with delight at being allowed out after dark. It was probably not long past supper time, but I felt that it must be midnight at least – *the witching hour*. The darkness danced with spectres.

We wrapped ourselves up in blankets and huddled together on the clifftop, the four standing stones looming around us. Pa lit the brandy in the snapdragon bowl and the flames flickered dangerously, casting shadows on our faces. I had never played the game before. My father and sister started swaying backwards and forwards, grinning and chanting together: 'Snip! Snap! Dragon!' They pinched the burning raisins from the flames. I did not recognize these strange, chanting, nightmarish creatures. I was half-afraid of them. I caught the rhythm of their words and joined in the game, pinching at the weird blue flames and gobbling up the burning-hot raisins.

With his blue and lapping tongue
Many of you will be stung!
Snip! Snap! Dragon!

After the game, when the flames had dwindled and our faces were lit only by the lantern, Pa told us the story of the standing stones.

'Long, long ago,' he said, his face suddenly serious and skull-like in the lamplight, 'a thick fog settled on this coast. It was very bad for the fishermen and their families, as they could not fish while the fog lingered, but it was even worse for the families of those aboard the *Aurora*. The *Aurora* had set out on the morning before the fog came, and she had still not returned.

'There were four men aboard the *Aurora* and each of these men had a daughter. Each evening the girls climbed the path from the harbour hand in hand, making their way up to this very clifftop to light the signal fire, and they kept the fire burning all through the long, cold nights. They hoped that, if the *Aurora* was still afloat, if she was lost somewhere in the fog, the bright flames would help to lead the little boat home. By the fourth evening, everyone else in the village had given up. They said the *Aurora* must have been swallowed by the Wyrm – the treacherous sandbank that lurked in the shadow of the towering cliffs. The Wyrm had wrecked many hundreds of ships over the centuries, and it was hungry for another sacrifice.

'But the girls had one last hope. That night, as usual, they wound their way up the cliff path hand in hand. As usual, they lit the fire, and tended it, and they sat and watched and waited for their fathers to return, but on this night they did not make their way home again.

'Here in the dark, on this very spot where we are sitting now, the girls sang a special song to the sea. They sang the sweetest, saddest song that has ever been heard. It was a song of love and loyalty and sacrifice, promising the greatest of gifts if only the *Aurora* were returned safely to the harbour. They sat and sang, and as they sang, they saw the fog begin to disperse. They kept singing and singing.

'Soon it was dawn and the girls stood up together, holding hands as the darkness dissolved and the new sun started to rise over the sea. Their white dresses billowed like sails in the first breeze that had blessed the shores in four long days and nights. A ghostly little boat seemed to bob up from the grey waves, and the girls knew it was the *Aurora*. They kept singing – but singing with joy now as they watched the fishing boat sail towards the harbour below.

'The Wyrm squirmed beneath the surface of the water. It had returned the *Aurora*, but now it felt angry and cheated and hungry. So it took the great sacrifice the girls had promised: it took their souls. Tentacles of mist reached up from the sea, creeping over the edge of the cliff and into their hearts. As the sun rose over the glittering water, the four daughters turned to stone.'

I shivered horribly. I felt all icy and strange. I looked

at Mags and she was frozen, her mouth hanging open. For a moment, I thought perhaps she had been turned to stone too, but then she blinked and swallowed. Pa was still talking, though his voice was very, very soft now – just a whisper.

'People say that the Daughters of Stone stand here on our clifftop as a warning to those who sail these dangerous waters. If you close your eyes and listen very carefully, you might just be able to hear their sad, sweet, ghostly song . . .'

A sea mist must have risen as Pa was telling the story; tendrils of it seemed to be creeping across the cliff. I was aware of the four stones surrounding us, watching us. I could almost hear them breathing. My heart was thudding in my throat now. I heard a whispered song, as soft as the hiss of sea foam over pebbles, the swish of a sea breeze through a long white dress.

For my father and sister, the legend of the Wyrm and the Stones was just that – a legend, distant through the mists of centuries. But for me it was different. From the moment I first heard the story, I knew it was much, much more. I knew it in the chill of my bone marrow and the crawling of my skin. I knew that the ancient magic of our cliffs was real and that I was destined – somehow – to become part of the legend too.

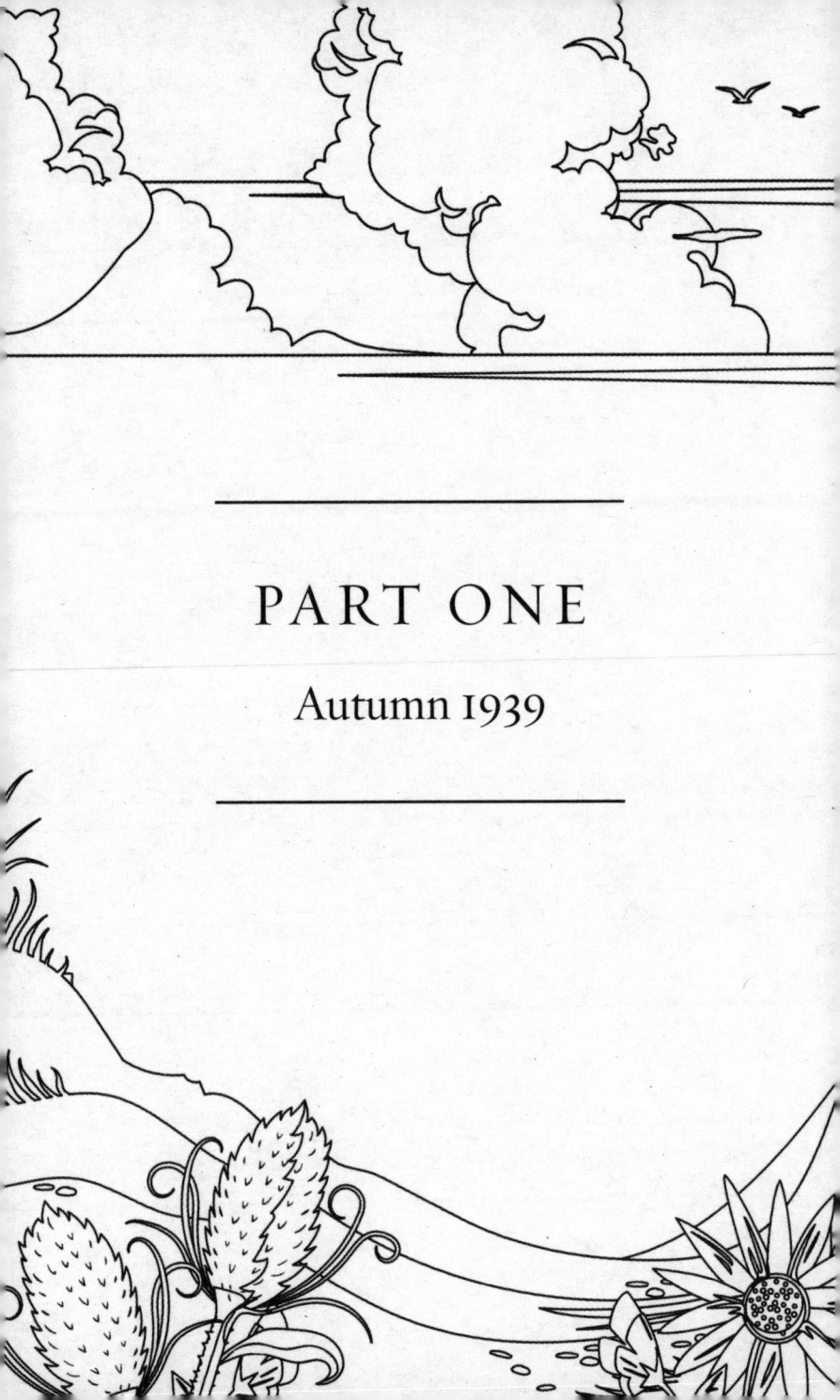

PART ONE

Autumn 1939

I

On the very first day of the war, Mags came home with a split lip. Her eye socket was swollen too and promised to ripen into a large, plum-coloured bruise. Her knuckles were red and grazed.

'What happened, Mags?' I gasped. 'Was it one of the girls at school?' But my sister ignored me, storming down the footpath and into the cottage through the kitchen door.

Mags is a fiery sort of person. Living with her is a bit like living with a half-tamed tornado, but for all her fierce temper she had never been in a proper fight before. Mutti made her sit down at the kitchen table. She gently bathed my sister's eye, lip and knuckles with warm water and witch hazel.

I hovered just inside the door, watching.

'Tell me who did this, please, Magda,' my mother said.

'It doesn't really matter who did it,' Mags muttered. 'It could have been any of them. They were all saying the same thing.'

'What? What were they saying?'

But Mags just drew in a long, shaky breath and would say nothing.

I could see Mutti's eyes were brimming with tears. She blinked them back, wiped her hands on her apron and then got on with preparing dinner. She pushed her hair from her face with her forearm and quickly chopped an onion. I wondered if she really needed to chop an onion for dinner, or if she just wanted to have something to blame her tears on.

Pa took Mags outside into the darkening garden and I followed a little way behind. I picked up the watering can and made myself look busy tending the vegetables.

Mags and Pa stood near the fence at the bottom of the garden, talking quietly – or rather, Pa was talking quietly and Mags was just staring at the ground with her arms folded across her chest. She kicked at the grass with the toe of one shoe. After a while I heard her say, 'You didn't hear them, Pa. You didn't hear what they said about Mutti.'

There's something I should mention about my family and, specifically, about Mutti – why we call her

Mutti and not Mum or Mother. Mutti was born in Germany and grew up there. German is her first language, and she's taught it to us too. *Mutter* is German for 'mother'. The fact that our Mutti had been born in Germany was never important to us – it was just normal, as normal to us as living in a lighthouse – but now that the war had started, other people seemed to think it was very important indeed.

Mutti called us all in to dinner, and we sat around the kitchen table in silence. Mags touched the corner of her lip and inspected her finger to see if it was still bleeding. It wasn't like a normal dinner time. There was something else at the table with us – something tense and waiting, like a gun that had been cocked but not yet fired – the fizzing gunpowder trail of the conversation Pa and Mags had started but not finished.

My sister had a library book in her lap – *Essential Motor Boat Maintenance* – but her eyes didn't seem to be focusing on the pages as she turned them over.

Pa moved his chair closer to Mags and leant towards her a little. She pretended to be interested in a diagram of a propeller. Mutti and I pretended to be interested in our dinner. Mags frowned down at her book, refusing to look at Pa.

'You're too old for playground scraps, Magda,' he said. 'You're nearly sixteen now.' Then he sighed, and when he spoke again his voice was softer. 'Try to let it go, Mags,' he said. 'Next time they start saying things like that, just try to let it go.'

Mags said nothing.

'You have a *choice*,' he went on. 'You don't have to react.'

'You're right, Pa,' Mags said at last, closing her book and turning to look him dead in the eye. 'I have a choice.'

And the conversation was over.

After dinner, Mags shut herself in our bedroom. She wanted to be by herself, so I took my sketchbook up to the lantern room. *Perhaps I'll draw the sunset*, I thought. There were some wonderfully dramatic clouds that evening – dark and jagged against the red sky.

You can see the Daughters of Stone from the top of our lighthouse. In fact, it feels as if you can see the whole world from up here. On a clear day the outline of the French coast is just visible on the other side of the broad, yawning Channel. The harbour is down there to the right, and our village, Stonegate, is tucked away just behind it, in the lee of the cliffs. When the tide is out you can just see Dragon Bay – that long, thin, sandy beach below the chalky south cliff that runs most of the way from here to Dover. If you turn and look the other way, the English farmland stretches out in an enormous patchwork of green and gold – hundreds of oddly-shaped fields all stitched together with hedgerows and dark woodland. Little groups of houses cluster around church spires, clinging to the roads that thread between the fields.

Because there are windows all the way around the lantern room, you can keep turning and turning, and soon the sea and fields, sea and fields, sea and fields become a blue-green blur and you have to sit down.

If you go through the door and out on to the walkway, and if you are brave enough to look down, you will see the standing stones beneath you. The wind out there is nearly always fierce and blustering, even in the summer. The four stones wrap around the seaward side of the lighthouse, like part of an enormous clock face, half-buried in the turf of the clifftop. I think the stones are the main reason that our lighthouse has always been known as the Castle. From a distance, the Daughters of Stone seem to be buttresses or guard towers, or even stony sentinels, facing out towards the sea and the storms, watching for enemies.

I had always liked the fact that there were four standing stones, just like the four of us – Mutti and Pa, Mags and me. The symmetry pleased me – each of us had our own stone. The smallest one was mine – furthest to the left, pointed at the top like a diamond. When we were little, Mags and I would pretend the stones were mountains to climb, or islands in a sea churning with predators – and we would use ropes and rocks and bits of wood to get from one stone to the next without getting our legs bitten off. I remember Mags brandishing a toy sword, using it to slash at the slimy tentacles that had twisted around me and were dragging me down into the inky, blood-black depths of the ocean . . . Pa told us to be careful. He said the stones were *megaliths* – they were thousands of years old, and if we wanted them to last another thousand years, we probably shouldn't be scrabbling about all over them.

Pa said people who were experts on megaliths had all sorts of theories about the stones – ideas to do with druids and rituals and the summer solstice. They believed the stones must have come from another part of England altogether, or maybe even France; they aren't local rock, as our cliffs are chalky and these stones glitter with granite.

I've dozed in the long grass between the stones on many a summer's afternoon. I've lain there for hours, listening to the lullaby of the sea and watching the slowly dimming sky. Mags doesn't believe me, but I've heard them singing – on those still, dark dawns when the sun struggles to rise through the fret or the fog. It's a strange, distant ghost-song, high and resonant, like four different tuning forks buzzing their soft notes from deep within the rock. It feels as if they are singing only to me.

Sometimes I speak to the stones – a sort of whis-pered, pagan prayer. I remember doing that on the evening of Magda's fight. As I drew their four, rain-rounded shapes and the dark daggers of cloud that hung above them, I asked the stones to protect my Mutti and my Pa, and my stupid, surly sister.

I have always believed that the Daughters somehow guarded our Castle, and in a way I think they do, but I know now that it is much more complicated than that. This sort of old magic is not loyal to anyone or anything. It has its own laws. It is as cold and unknowable as an ancient god.

2

It was just a few days after Magda's fight that Pa received a very strange order from the government. We had to paint the Castle green.

We all painted it together. Pots of green paint shot up and down on pulleys and I was allowed to use the stepladder to paint the downstairs windowsills. It was much better than whitewashing, because if we splashed paint on the grass, it didn't matter so much – you could hardly see it. Mags painted the very top of the lighthouse – the round roof. She scaled the highest part of the tower with a rope, just like a mountain climber, her paintbrush tucked in a back pocket. It took the four of us three whole days to paint it, and the closer it was to being finished, the more peculiar it looked. I couldn't get used to the greeny-brown paint at all – it just looked completely the wrong colour for a lighthouse.

'It's camouflage,' Pa said. 'To make us harder to spot from the air. We don't want the lighthouse to be bombed, do we?'

No. We didn't.

There has been a lighthouse above Stonegate for centuries – to warn ships of the dangerous sandbank in the sea beyond the cliffs, and to guide them safely past the Wyrm to the harbour below. Its light has come from all sorts of different things, from oil lamps to braziers and coal fires. It hasn't always looked the same, of course, but I was pretty sure that it had never been painted green before. The lighthouse has been destroyed many times. It has been hit by hurricanes, struck by lightning and burnt down by fire, but it has always risen again – a phoenix from the storm-blown flames.

I love our lighthouse, and I couldn't imagine living anywhere else, but I know that other people often find it odd. They might imagine, perhaps, that all the furniture has to be round in order to fit inside, or that we sleep in hammocks hung from the spiral staircase, and spend our days climbing ladders and polishing glass. Actually, there is a fair bit of glass-polishing that has to be done, but we have never slept in hammocks: we sleep in normal beds in the cottage at the foot of the lighthouse. The cottage is just like any other cottage really, like any other home. And we are just like any other family. At least, we *were* just like any other family, before the war began. Now, if I think back to that sunny autumn day when we finished painting the lighthouse, I can see that the tide had already begun to turn.

It was beautifully warm for September, and Mags and I lay next to each other in the long grass between the standing stones.

'Looks odd, doesn't it?' Mags said. 'Now that it's green.'

'It looks weird,' I agreed.

I loved our strong, white tower – brilliant and proud against a clear blue sky. It looked so different now that it was the same sort of earthy colour as the fields that surrounded us. It looked as if it had sprouted up from the ground itself.

'It looks like a goblin castle,' I said.

Mags laughed. 'Or an ogre's folly.'

'Or a troll's tower.'

My sister plucked a daisy and threw it at my face. I laughed too and closed my eyes. My muscles were achy from painting, and the grass was warm and dry and pleasantly scratchy beneath me.

'It makes sense, though, doesn't it?' Mags said in a more serious voice. 'Hitler's bombers won't be able to spot us as easily now. Pa said there is a risk that landmarks like lighthouses could be used by German planes for navigation.'

'Mmmm.' I started to feel very sleepy. I listened to the gulls calling to each other as they wheeled over the waves. The sea air up on the cliffs was soft, sun-warmed and seaweedy – completely different from the cold-salt smell of the sea in winter. I thought dreamily that the people in Germany were breathing the same gentle air as us, and I wondered if there was a little German girl, lying in the grass somewhere, thinking about me. I stuck my hands up in the air and squinted at them, spreading my fingers out and examining the splashes of green paint on my skin.

Then I heard the engines.

A weird thing happens to me when I am frightened. I freeze. Like a startled rabbit. My whole body stiffens and I can't move at all. People use the word 'petrified' to describe feeling afraid, but it really means much more than that – it means being so terrified that you cannot move a muscle; it means being turned to stone.

I lay there, rigid, breathing very quickly, while the noise of the aeroplane came closer and closer.

'Pa!' Mags shouted.

Everything darkened around me.

3

There were footsteps then, pounding footsteps. Pa was pelting across the garden, and he had picked me up and flung me over his shoulder before I knew what was happening. He ran back to the cottage with Mags at his side, and I went bump, bump, bump, dangling upside down and watching the jolting colours of the sky behind us. 'All right, Pet?' Pa called. My family often called me Pet – a silly, shortened version of my name, Petra. 'Pet' was affectionate, I knew, but it always made me feel small – like a toy dog on a lead, or a mouse in a cage. I felt pathetic as I hung there, bouncing around like a sack of potatoes on my father's back.

The engines buzzed louder and louder in the sky above, until it felt as if the whole world were burning with noise. Mutti was waiting for us at the door of the cottage. From upside down, she looked quite normal, but when I was turned the right way up, I could see how scared she was. Pa was calmer; his face was like a slab of stone. 'It's the first,' he said. 'It's just the first, and it probably won't be the last. Reconnaissance, I expect,' he said. That meant they were enemy planes coming over to gather information.

Pa said we had to go down to the coal cellar. We were to come here whenever we heard low-flying aeroplanes or caught the sound of the air-raid siren drifting up from Stonegate harbour below. Mags said that she thought most of the planes would probably be ours. By 'ours' she meant British planes.

'Yes, they probably will,' Pa said. 'And we'll learn to tell the difference. But for now, we won't know which is which until it's too late.'

That was the first time I really understood that the war had started and that we and our lighthouse were in danger. But I still felt safe. As we descended into the dusty dark of the coal cellar together, I felt so very, very safe.

Mutti tried to encourage me to curl up in an old armchair and go to sleep, but I wanted to poke about amongst the piles of bric-a-brac stacked up in the cobwebby corners. The smell of coal dust and mould was mysterious and exciting. I started clambering through a stack of broken furniture – I was an insect in a dusty jungle.

'Be careful please, little Pet,' Mutti said. 'That furniture is very old – you will hurt yourself.' I was twelve years old. I wondered just how old I would have to be before I stopped being Mutti's 'little Pet'.

I stopped climbing and stood quietly for a minute or so, writing my name in the dust that covered an old writing desk. *Pet Smith*, I wrote. Then I wrote my full name (including my middle name that comes from Mutti's family): *Petra Zimmermann Smith*.

That is the name of someone extraordinary, I thought. *An explorer. An adventurer, or a mountain climber. Someone who does wonderful and fearless things.* I wasn't brave enough to be an adventurer, though, I knew that. I wasn't bold and fearless like Magda. What I really wanted was to be an artist. I sighed, and stared at my name. I had always felt it was several sizes too big for me. Was it a name I could grow into? I scribbled it out and wrote plain *Pet Smith* again. I was anonymous once more – small, mousey and unimportant.

I started looking through the desk drawers one at a time, to see if I could find any little bits of forgotten treasure. Apart from a few dead earwigs they all seemed to be empty. Everyone was quiet. Mags lay down on an old mattress with her book clasped to her chest. I watched her close her eyes tightly, but I knew she wasn't asleep – her breathing was all wrong. Pa sat next to Mutti and took her hand. I saw my mother stealing glances at Mags every now and then – she'd been watching her like that since the fight earlier that week. After a while Mags opened her eyes and huffed impatiently, as if Mutti's anxious looks were keeping her awake. She moved beneath the fanlight and opened *Essential Motor Boat Maintenance*, squinting at the pages as the last dregs of evening light faded into darkness. I caught the faintest trace of the air-raid siren in the wind, still wailing mournfully from the village below.

Pa was restless. He got up and lit a couple of oil lamps, and the yellow light illuminated something at the back of a desk drawer I had thought to be empty. I took it out and dusted it with my sleeve. It was a photograph in a frame – a formal photograph of a bride and groom on their wedding day. A vicar was standing beside them. I looked closely at the faces of the couple. She was a young woman with long, yellow-brown hair just like mine. She was wearing a simple dress with a pattern of leaves on it, and holding a bouquet of wild flowers. He was a gentle-looking man with sticking-out ears, wearing his only good suit.

It is Mutti and Pa. I'd know Pa's ears anywhere . . .

I recognized one of the other figures – the old lady who stood beside the bride was Mrs Fisher from the village. She was dead now, but she used to do the flowers at the village church and was a cousin or aunt of Mutti's (Mutti worked in her hotel when she first came over to England from Germany). Mrs Fisher was easy to recognize because she always wore a hat covered in large artificial sunflowers. A thin man stood beside her. He had fair hair, an angular face and a neat, pointed beard. He was holding a plate piled high with wedding cake.

I wanted to show the photograph to Mutti and Pa, but something told me not to. There were three things about the photograph that struck me as being very important and very strange:

1. It was Mutti and Pa's wedding day, but there only seemed to be two guests.
2. No one in the photograph was smiling.
3. The photograph had been hidden away in the coal cellar.

I put it back and gently closed the desk drawer, leaving it where I had found it — amongst the rubbish and the dust and all the other forgotten things.

4

It seemed wrong not to tell Mags about the wedding photograph straight away – I had always told my sister everything, but for some reason I wanted to keep this as my secret, at least for the time being. I sensed that there was a mystery attached to the picture – a secret reason for it being hidden away like that – and I wanted to solve the puzzle myself, without Mags taking over.

She knew that there was something on my mind. That night, she whispered to me from her bed, 'Are you all right, Pet? Are you scared about an air raid or something?'

'I'm fine,' I replied.

'No, you're not,' she insisted. 'I can always tell when you're lying, Pet. Sisters always know.'

'I'm fine,' I said again.

She *hmphed* quietly, and I heard her bed creak as she rolled over towards the blacked-out window. I was aware of an odd, new distance opening up between us.

Now that I think about it, it was around this time that Mags started to behave strangely. She muttered in her sleep, and one morning I caught her in a sort of trance, sitting on the edge of her bed with one sock on and one sock off, staring dreamily at the wall. When I asked her if she was all right, she snapped at me to leave her alone. So I did. I plodded up the lighthouse stairs with my sketchbook and pencil and sat in the lantern room. I felt the need to draw something, but I ended up just thinking about the hidden photograph and doodling a pattern of waves.

It was one of those grey, heavy autumn days when endless banks of cloud roll in from the horizon, and the sun never quite manages to take hold. I watched a boy come up the cliff path towards our cottage, carrying a brown paper parcel. As he got closer, I realized it was Kipper Briggs – a boy from the village. Kipper is as big as a man, broad-backed and large-handed. He was the same age as Mags, though he had left school a couple of years ago to work for his father (Arthur Briggs was the fishmonger in the village and he owned half a dozen fishing boats, which used to head out of the harbour every morning come rain or shine).

I watched Kipper climb the last, steep stretch of the path and come through our garden gate. It banged shut behind him, and a seagull flapped haphazardly across the garden, startled by the noise. I put down my sketchbook and pencil and ran down the stairs to meet him; he was probably bringing Mutti's order of fish for the week.

Kipper is not a pleasant boy to be around, I'm afraid – and I'm not just talking about his aroma (children can be very inventive when it comes to cruel nicknames, but whoever christened Colin Briggs 'Kipper' didn't need much of an imagination – only a basic sense of smell). Kipper used to be famous for stealing the lunches of the smallest children at school. I remember him taking an iced bun from Mags, and gobbling it up right in front of her furious face. Mags had only been about ten years old at the time, and Kipper must have been much bigger than her, but she'd kicked him in the shins for that.

By the time I had run down the lighthouse stairs, I was a bit dizzy. Rather than going through the cottage, I came out of the main lighthouse door and stopped for a second, holding on to the door frame to steady myself. There were two figures standing by the garden gate – Mags must have seen Kipper coming too, and she'd got there before me. I don't know who had said what to whom in the short time it had taken me to get down the stairs, but it didn't take me long to realize that they were on the brink of a fight.

'Don't know why Dad's still doing business with you lot of crummy krauts,' Kipper was sniping. Mags held out her hand for the parcel, but Kipper kept it just out of reach. He danced around her. 'Oh, you want this, do you, Jerry? Come and get it . . .'

Mags's face didn't even flicker, and she didn't try to grab the parcel; she wasn't playing Kipper's game. She folded her arms, keeping eye contact with Kipper. She looked almost bored, but I know Mags, and I knew her heart would have been thundering.

'Come on,' Kipper taunted, backing out through the gate again. 'Come and get it, Magda . . . Or are you *scared*?'

'I'm not scared of you, Kipper,' Mags said evenly. 'But I *am* afraid of getting too close — I just can't stand the smell, I'm afraid.'

'Oh, you think you're funny, don't you, *Frau Smeeth*! You think you're *it*. Up here in your so-called *castle*. Think you're better than us, don't you? Well, you're not. If you don't take that back, I'm going to lob your parcel right off the ruddy cliff!'

It was at this point that Kipper, now reversing quickly towards the cliff edge, his eyes fixed on Mags, collided with our enormous ginger cat Barnaby. Barnaby yowled and tore back towards the cottage, and Kipper started falling backwards, his arms wind-milling wildly. He was heading for the edge of the cliff and I shrieked before starting towards him, along with Mags, who was already halfway there. At the very last moment, Kipper's foot went down a rabbit hole and he fell, not backwards towards the edge, but to his left, cracking the side of his head on one of the standing stones.

'Are you all right, Kipper?' I called.

Mags laughed. It wasn't a cruel laugh as such – more relief than anything, I think – but it made Kipper even angrier. Now he was humiliated too. 'You'll be sorry!' he snarled at us both, as if we had done this to him on purpose. He pushed himself up, blinking back tears and clutching the side of his head. 'You'll be sorry! Everyone knows what you all are – and everyone knows what you're up to!' He stumbled towards the cliff path and flung the dirty parcel towards us. It landed soggily at my feet. 'She's been seen!' he spat. He pointed a trembling finger towards the lighthouse. 'My dad told me – he's *seen* her. And I'm going to make sure everyone knows.' Then he finally turned and limped away.

We were both silent for a moment. The clouds over the sea were as heavy as boulders. I could see a thin, dark line of liquid trickling down the standing stone where Kipper's head had cracked against it.

'Seen who, Mags?' I breathed, not daring to look up at my sister. 'What was he talking about?'

'He's talking rubbish, Petra,' she muttered.

'Kipper's an idiot. Just ignore him.'

But, as she turned back towards the cottage, I saw that my sister's face was white as chalk.

5

We didn't see Kipper again until the day the gas masks arrived. What a horrible day that was – and what a horrible thing a gas mask is. I know it could save my life, of course – I'm not stupid. I just can't help finding it terrifying. Sometimes I can feel my gas mask looking at me from its home on the kitchen sideboard – with its round, glassy, goggle eyes, and its round mouth too – fixed in an O of horror. It is always there, ready to be strapped on in an ugly, rubbery panic should the moment ever come.

We were summoned to collect our gas masks just a few weeks after the blackout started. Everyone queued up in the village hall and we were issued with a mask one at a time, while the vicar's wife ticked our names off her list with a blunt pencil. Then we all had to sit down in rows.

There must have been about fifty of us there in the village hall that day. Kipper Briggs sat at the back with his father and, when I turned around to look at him, he raised his chin and just glared past me towards the front of the hall, where Mrs Baron, our headmistress, was demonstrating how the gas masks worked.

I remember watching Mrs Baron as she was speaking to us all, and deciding that if she were a bird, she would probably be a kestrel. She was wearing her usual tweed suit with a pearl-coloured scarf around her neck. Her hair was done up in a neat bronze twist, and her narrow grey eyes darted about as she spoke. Mrs Baron was probably the busiest lady in Stonegate. She and her son Michael had moved to our village from London about three years ago and she had swiftly become what Pa called 'a pillar of the community'. Not only was she the headmistress of our school but she was also a magistrate at the court in Dover.

'So,' she was saying, 'I shall, for the time being at least, be the village's Air Raid Precaution, or ARP, warden.'

'What?' a voice called out rudely from the back. 'ARP warden? *As well as* headmistress and Justice of the flamin' Peace?' It was Arthur Briggs, Kipper's father.

'Yes, Arthur,' Mrs Baron replied, deploying the tolerant smile she usually reserved for the children who shouted out stupid things in class. 'Unless you fancy the job, of course?'

'You're welcome to it, I'm sure,' muttered Briggs, adding a sarcastic 'M'lady' under his breath. Then I heard him mutter to Kipper, 'Fingers in too many pies, that one . . . She'll be Queen of flamin' England next.'

Very wisely, Mrs Baron chose to ignore Arthur Briggs and was now pressing on with instructions on how to use the gas masks, but I found it very difficult to concentrate, because Mags was fanning herself, flapping her gas mask instructions right next to my face, and it kept making me blink. She seemed to be in a sort of trance, staring intently towards the front of the hall. I nudged her, and when she eventually looked at me, I swatted her gas mask instructions right out of her hand. Mags scowled and elbowed me hard in the ribs, making me squeak. I was immediately aware that Mrs Baron had stopped talking and was looking straight at me. My stomach went tight. Other people were turning to look at me now too.

'This is no laughing matter, young lady,' she said, pressing her lips together and shaking her head in disappointment. 'This device could save your life, you know. Come along, Petra. Come up here and I'll show you how it works.'

I squeezed past Mags, out of our row, and made my way to the front of the hall to stand beside Mrs Baron. I felt like a magician's assistant about to be sawn in half. I hoped no one could see that my knees were shaking.

I had always rather liked Mrs Baron, but right now she was my least favourite person on the whole planet – after Mags, of course. I glared at my sister and tried not to make eye contact with Mutti and Pa, who were smiling at me proudly as if I had been picked to play the lead part in the school play. I noticed Mrs Baron's handsome sixteen-year-old son Michael was also smiling, and I hoped that my cheeks weren't too beet-root-red.

Then I realized that Mrs Baron's eagle-eyes had settled expectantly upon me and I hadn't been listening to a single word she had been saying.

'Off you go, Petra,' she said, gesturing to the mask I was clutching in my hands.

I knew exactly what was going to happen next. What always happened to me when I was this frightened. I froze.

Mrs Baron sighed. 'Like this, dear . . .' And quite suddenly she had taken the gas mask out of my rigid hands, pressed it on to my face and was pulling the tight strap over the top of my head.

I was underwater. I was drowning.

The village hall became a sinking ship, swaying its way down to the bottom of the deepest, greenest sea, taking me and everyone else with it. My whole head was pinched with pressure and I gasped for air, hearing a strange, alien hiss as I managed to draw in a little dizzying oxygen, just enough to keep me alive for a few agonizing seconds, until, at last, I felt a hand on the back of my head pulling the strap off again – and then – oh, the relief! – I could breathe once more – I could move! I folded in half, hands on my shaking knees, tongue hanging out of my mouth, trying to inhale enough clean air to get rid of the bitter, rubbery taste of the mask.

'Are you all right, Petra?' Mrs Baron said, rubbing my back soothingly. 'It is a bit odd at first, I know, but don't worry – you'll get used to it with practice!' She gave a sympathetic little laugh and everyone else in the village hall laughed too.

My face burnt with embarrassment as I made my way unsteadily out of the door along with the rest of the village, my gas mask safely back in its cardboard box. I took a deep, cool breath of the seaside air and turned my face up towards the sun, as if its light could some-how bleach away the horror of the last few minutes.

'You did well, Petra,' said a voice beside me. I turned to see Michael Baron's sparkling green eyes looking down at me. 'I felt quite queasy the first time I tried to breathe through one of these. Tastes horrible, doesn't it?'

'Disgusting,' I agreed, and started to feel a bit better, but then I was knocked sideways by my idiotic sister bumping into me. Michael gave us both a cheer-ful wink before he turned left and started striding off up the hill.

'Thanks for nothing, Mags,' I hissed through gritted teeth.

She just gave me a sarcastic little grin.

Michael turned back then and called to us: 'By the way, are you two ladies entering the crabbing competition tomorrow?'

'I didn't think it was happening this year,' Magda replied.

'Of course it's happening — not going to let a silly little thing like a war get in the way of an important tradition like crabbing, are you?'

Mags laughed.

'And it'll be fun beating Kipper again . . .' Michael timed this remark beautifully, just as Kipper and his father emerged from the village hall. 'Calls himself a fisherman, but last year he couldn't even catch a cold, could you, Kipper?'

Kipper glared at Michael and started to turn away. But Mr Briggs went crimson. He shoved Kipper forward with a snarl, as if encouraging his son to fight Michael Baron on the spot, but Kipper shrugged him off, stuck his hands in his pockets and sloped off down the hill towards the harbour. After spitting on the cobbles, and cursing 'the flamin' high and mighty Barons', his father followed him.

Michael raised his eyes to heaven and grinned. 'Well, I'll see you bright and early tomorrow, then, ladies!' he called over his shoulder.

'*Crabbing*, Mags?' I said. 'Do we have to?'

'Of course!' she insisted, smiling broadly. 'It's a tradition! Come on, Pet. We'll take the rowing boat and a picnic – it'll be fun.'

I didn't really want to go, but I could see it was suddenly important to Mags, and she hadn't looked this happy about anything since the war had begun.

'Fine,' I grumbled. 'Just promise me you won't get too competitive about it. I don't want to be drifting about in the boat for hours and hours until it gets dark.' Just the thought of it made me feel cold and sick.

'I promise,' she said. But she had that wild, excited look in her eye.

I should have known then that something was going to go wrong.

6

'We're too far out, Mags – there aren't any crabs here.'

'Don't be daft,' my sister said. 'This is where you find the really big ones, Pet. Just drop your line a bit lower.'

I looked in the bucket at our collection of dead-eyed, razor-clawed creatures, all spider-legged and snapping and clambering over each other. I shuddered. I didn't want to catch any *really big ones*.

'Let's try here.' Mags pulled on the left oar and reversed with the right, skilfully spinning us around so that we faced away from the coast and towards the open sea. The water was different out here – darker, deeper; it whirlpooled thickly around the oars.

I glanced back towards Dragon Bay. Most of the

children from the village were out in little boats, just like us, dangling their crabbing lines into the water. We were the furthest out, though, by a long way; their shouts of laughter were distant. I had a bad feeling about this.

'We're getting too close to the Wyrm, Mags,' I said, aware that my voice sounded childish and complaining.

'The sandbank? That won't do us any harm, Pet,' she insisted. 'We're in a rowing boat, not a galleon. We're not going to capsize or anything. The worst that will happen is that we'll get grounded for a while until the tide rises again.'

'Brilliant,' I muttered under my breath. I fixed the next scrap of bacon rind on to my line, silently cursing my competitive sister. She was always getting me into ridiculous scrapes. The idea of being stranded on the back of the Wyrm sent a pang of fear through my stomach.

Some people think the sandbank is called the Wyrm because you have to learn its twists and turns if you want to sail this coast: you have to 'worm' your way around the cliffs to the harbour. But Pa told us that *wyrm* is the Old English word for dragon. So many ships were wrecked here over the centuries that sailors used to believe the sandbank was actually a sea dragon that lurked beneath the waves, waiting patiently for sacrifices to sail into its path. It would overturn each ship with a flip of its scaly tail, before twisting around to swallow it whole.

I have a very cruel imagination. In my darkest, most lonely moments, it likes to torture me by playing out the most frightening things I have ever seen or heard. Since Pa first told me the legend of our coast, I had developed a recurring nightmare about the Wyrm. It didn't suck my soul into the sea or turn me to stone like it did to the Daughters; instead, it crawled right out of the water to get me. In my nightmare, the Wyrm was a real, hungry sea dragon, with rows of needle-sharp teeth that reeked of rotten fish. And it wanted to eat me alive. I saw it emerge from the waves, its scaled skin pale, translucent and dripping wet. It hissed and dripped and clawed its way up the cliffs to the Castle. I ran as fast as I could, into the lighthouse and up the stairs until I found myself in the lantern room – panting and shaking – and there was nowhere else to run to. I always tried to hide, but I knew it was no use. The Wyrm was coming for me. I would be its next sacrifice. The most terrifying thing about this dream was the noise – the slow, wet footsteps; the scraping of its scales against the walls as it squeezed its way up the narrow stairs; the hissing of its foul breath as it got closer and closer, and I couldn't move . . .

I always woke up just before the Wyrm actually appeared in the lantern room, though. Always.

I took a deep breath of sea air and tried to force the hideous Wyrm out of my mind. I looked towards our

Castle – a dark silhouette on the clifftop above us. The Daughters of Stone seemed to glitter in the soft, white light, and I felt my heart become a little calmer. I measured out an extra few yards on my crabbing line and started to lower the bacon rind into the water.

'Longer than that,' Mags said.

'You do the rowing, I'll do the fishing,' I said, turning to look her in the eye. My sister was wearing one of Mutti's winter hats, her brown hair peeking out from beneath it in glossy curls. She didn't normally wear a hat when she went out rowing or sailing – her hair was usually a tangled, salty, windswept mess, and Mutti despaired of ever getting the knots out of it. 'Why are you wearing a hat today, Mags?' I asked. 'It's not cold.'

'I just felt like it,' she said unconvincingly. She pulled the hat down a bit more, suddenly self-conscious.

'Is it to keep your ears in?' I teased. Mags had inherited Pa's most distinctive feature.

'Shut up, Pet,' she snapped, pulling hard on the left oar again. She was fighting the current.

'*Sorry*,' I muttered. Her sticking-out ears had never bothered her before. Why was she suddenly worried about them now?

I leant over the side of the boat to try to see if the bait was dropping deeply enough. She was right – I did need to let out a bit more line, and I probably needed to add a bit more weight too, to get it to sink rather than drifting with the current. I watched the white scrap of meat slowly disappearing through the depths of murky water.

Thinking about Pa's sticking-out ears made me think about the hidden wedding photograph again. *Perhaps I should mention it to Mags after all*, I thought. It would be a mystery we could solve together. It might even help to close that strange gap that seemed to be opening up between us. If nothing else, it would stop thoughts of the Wyrm from slithering back into my head.

I was just about to say something when Mags shouted, 'What the hell is THAT?'

The fishing line dropped through my fingers. I had already got myself into a state by thinking too much about the Wyrm, so the effect of this sudden panic was rather like being harpooned with fear. I stood up to try to see what she was looking at but, before I knew it, she leant forwards, the boat gave a great lurch, and I was sent tumbling sideways. I made a frantic grab at the side of the boat – ripping my nails on the splintery wood – but it was too late: I was flying into the water. I gasped at the air and closed my eyes tightly, but nothing could have prepared me for the jolt of freezing salt water as it slapped my face and body and closed in all around me. I felt the sudden, sodden weight of my clothes dragging me down, and somehow managed to wriggle out of my woollen sweater. It was Pa's voice in my head, I think, calmly telling me what to do, but the rest of me was a terrified mess of panicking child. My legs were kicking helplessly in the water, my lungs were screaming. I could just hear Mags's muted voice above the surface – 'PET!' – and I kicked out again, craning my face upwards until at last the muffling roar of water popped clear in my ears and I felt air on my face. I took an enormous gasping breath, my eyes and nose and throat burning with salt-water.

'Pet – hold on!' Mags was reaching down towards me, and my slippery-fish hand found hers, strong and warm. But she couldn't pull me up high enough and the boat rocked towards me; she had to let go and I dropped back into the water again. 'Hold on to this!' She threw me a loop of coarse rope and I clung on to it. 'I'll move us closer to the sandbank, Pet, so you can stand up and climb back in.'

'NO!' I called, but it was too late – she was already heaving the boat around. My feet flailed helplessly, and I was aware of the fathoms of dark water beneath me – the fish and eels and monsters that lay, waiting, at the bottom of the sea. I imagined the Wyrm waking from a century-long slumber, sniffing at the water, turning hungrily in my direction, reaching up with its filthy claws, opening its jaws of needle-pointed teeth . . . Something brushed against my foot and I screamed. My breathing was ragged and choking – 'Get me out, Mags! Get me OUT!' The cold water and the terror were freezing my limbs so that my fingers could barely keep their grip on the rope.

'Hold ON, Pet!'

I was the same as the lump of bacon rind, dangling there in the water: I was a piece of bait, and the foul jaws were about to close around me. Something was under my foot – something solid – I shrieked and kicked desperately against it, and found myself rising up against the hull. I pushed down again, pulling on the rope with numb hands, and I managed to get my head and chest over the side of the boat. I had one last terrifying vision of something dragging me back into the water before Mags grabbed my hand and hauled me all the way in.

We lay there in the bottom of the boat for a minute, catching our breath. The relief was overwhelming, and I felt tears welling up in my stinging eyes, sobs rising in my raw, burning throat. A shallow pool of seawater swilled gently up and down in the hull beneath us.

'Sorry, Pet,' Mags half-laughed. 'Are you all right?'

'All right,' I managed to say.

She took off her dry jumper and helped me into it. 'Keep warm,' she said. 'I'll take us back in.'

Just before we got to shore, Michael Baron's boat met us.

'I heard screaming – did you catch a whopper?' he asked. Then he saw me, all wet and shivering like a half-drowned kitten. 'Oh, dear,' he said. 'Man overboard?'

I nodded miserably.

'What happened?'

Mags answered: 'I saw something in the water and I moved to get a better look and—'

'And the boat wobbled, and Pet fell in?' Michael laughed. 'Poor little Pet. Never mind – you'll be home and all warm and dry before you know it.' Then he looked back at Mags. 'What did you see?'

'Sorry?'

'In the water. What did you see?'

Mags looked embarrassed for a second. 'I don't really know. Just this huge dark shape under the surface. I've never seen anything like it before.'

I started shaking again, but it wasn't because I was cold. *A monster*, I thought. There really was a monster out there – and it nearly got me.

Mags laughed a little. 'I thought it was a whale or something.'

'That big?' Michael looked at her with a strangely serious expression on his face. 'You know what it *could* have been, don't you, Mags?'

'What?'

His green eyes shone with boyish excitement. 'A German U-boat.'

7

Mags suggested that we tell the police, just in case that dark, sinister shape really had been a German U-boat, but Michael Baron said there was no point as they wouldn't believe us. He tried to persuade her to take him out in the boat straight away so that he could see it, but I fixed my sister with such an 'I'll tell Pa' look that she took me home instead.

I couldn't decide what was more horrifying – the idea that I'd stepped on to the scaled skin of the Wyrm in my struggle to get out of the water, or that what I'd felt beneath my feet had been the top of an enemy submarine.

There were certainly rumours of U-boats in the Channel. Some of the fishermen came home with stories of having spotted them lurking beneath the water, but most people dismissed the sightings, just as fishermen's tales of mermaids and sea serpents had been dismissed for thousands of years.

Could the enemy really be that close to our coast? Could they be watching us? Since those first reconnaissance planes on the day we finished painting the lighthouse, everything had been eerily quiet – no bombs or gas, none of the things we had been warned about – just air-raid drills and false alarms. Someone on the wireless had called it the 'Twilight War'. *Perhaps the promised darkness is never going to come*, I had thought. *Perhaps all the trouble is just going to fade quietly away* . . . But now it seemed possible that the darkness was much, much closer than we'd thought. I didn't know it at the time, but its shadowy fingers were already reaching into the very heart of my family.

A couple of months after the disastrous crabbing competition, a stubborn fog settled over Stonegate. Pa was under strict instructions not to light the lamp. He only lit it now when he received a telephone call, telling him that the light was needed for the safe passage of a particular British convoy. The foghorn was not sounded very often either – again, only when the telephone rang or Pa received a radio message. This was to make sure that we were not accidentally helping any enemy aeroplanes or vessels that might be near our coast.

On the third foggy morning, I was up in the lantern room writing the weather report in the logbook for Pa: *Temperature: 41°F*, I wrote. *Visibility: very poor . . .* I stared out at the sea of cloud that swirled below us, trying to estimate how many feet ahead I could see, but the fog moved in slow, white waves. It was as if the lighthouse were the bridge of a ship, and my Pa was the captain, sailing us all away from the real world, away from the war, out into the peace of the misty ocean . . . Then the telephone started ringing in the service room downstairs.

I stopped writing and listened. The telephone is only to be used by the lighthouse keeper. I'm not really supposed to know, but Mags told me it is a direct line to the Admiralty. A lighthouse keeper is a very important person in wartime — it is a reserved occupation, so you cannot be conscripted into the army.

I heard Pa's brief responses to whatever orders he was receiving, then the click and jingle of the telephone as he hung up. His footsteps descended the stairs. A moment later, the lighthouse door opened and closed as he went outside to the foghorn shed, and a few seconds later a deafening blast of sound. No matter how many times I heard the foghorn, it still made me jump. I squeezed my eyes shut — as if that would help somehow. *There must be a ship stranded in the Channel*, I thought. *Lost in the fog — drifting near the sandbank . . .* The sound stopped at last. Then I heard Pa coming up the spiral staircase, but he wasn't whistling as he usually did when he went up and down the stairs. His footsteps gradually became louder until he appeared in front of me in the lantern room. He looked very smart, as always, in his lighthouse-keeper's uniform. With his square shoulders, his neatly trimmed beard and his polished brass buttons, I thought he looked like an admiral in the Navy (albeit an admiral with sticking-out ears). He was carrying a very serious-looking envelope, which he tucked inside his jacket pocket. I saw that it had been opened and then closed again, the long edge folded tightly over.

'Top-Secret Lighthouse Keeper's Business?' I asked.

He hesitated for a moment, then he tapped his nose. 'Top. Secret,' he said. I felt a little surge of pride at how important my Pa was.

He consulted his watch. 'One minute, please, First Mate,' he said. 'Do you want to help?'

I smiled and saluted him. 'Aye, aye, Cap'n,' I said.

He passed me the heavy iron handle for the optic. I fitted the handle carefully and wound it around, bending my knees with each rotation to crank up the clockwork mechanism.

Pa counted under his breath, then he said, 'That should do it.'

Soundlessly, the optic started turning. It looked like a huge lampshade or drum with alternating panels of glass and wood — a giant zoetrope. As it rotated smoothly around the lamp, it gave the effect of the light flashing.

Pa pulled down the switch to light up the lantern and the beam of light shot out into the fog. We both watched the slow-flashing light as it attempted to penetrate the misty air. Each beam looked almost solid, I thought – a blinding-white rod of metal, a spear for a Greek god . . . Then there was a heavy click. I blinked, and the light had gone. The lantern seemed to glow for a moment – electric-orange, then red – and then the world was colourless once more.

Pa stood still for a while, his ocean-blue eyes fixed forward, as if in a trance. With the fading of the lamp, something seemed to have faded in him too. I stared out of the window, trying to catch a glimpse of the ship lost in the sea fret, but the world below was nothing but a smoky swamp.

Then, from somewhere out in the Channel, we heard the sound of a distant foghorn, and I felt an unexpected spasm of panic: *Are we helping the right ship?* Pa knew his job, of course; he knew his signals – but fear of the U-boat lurked just beneath the surface of my thoughts. What if the enemy had other vessels out there too, hiding in the fog?

The sound of the foghorn brought Pa out of his trance. He gave me a distracted little smile, kissed me on my forehead, then went back down the stairs. *There's something on his mind*, I thought. *He is very worried about something. Something important.* I wondered if it was connected to that envelope he had just put in his pocket.

Silently, I added this to the list of puzzles in my head: the hidden photograph, the dark shape in Dragon Bay, Kipper's accusation, my sister's weird behaviour . . . And now Pa. A whole shoal of secrets, writhing in my mind like fish in a net.

The fog did not lift all that day, and it was still there the next morning, cloaking the cliffs in stillness and secrecy. Our Castle was a castle lost in the clouds.

The chill seeped into my bones as I tiptoed from the front door of the cottage and out into the pearl-grey gloom.

I was following Mutti.

Mags had gone out early – probably down to the harbour to work on her boat, as she often did early in the mornings – and I had been lying there in bed, unable to get back to sleep. When I heard the kitchen door opening and closing again, I crept to the window, lifted the blackout blind and peered out into the mist. I could just make out Mutti's shadowy figure moving down the path towards the gate. What was she up to? It must have been around seven o'clock, and it was still quite dark. Mags sneaking out of the house to work on her boat was perfectly normal, but I'd never known Mutti to go for an early-morning walk – and certainly not in weather like this. And there was something about the way she had opened and closed the kitchen door. So softly . . .

I pulled the collar of my coat up and huffed into my scarf to try to keep my face warm. My hands were tightened into fists in my coat pocket and I wished I had taken a second to find my mittens. I trod carefully, trying not to make a sound. The figure of my mother was about twenty paces ahead of me. Every now and then the fog became so thick that I couldn't see her at all. We were out on the cliff path now. In the darkness and fog, so near the cliff edge, it would have been dangerous for anyone else, but I had grown up here – I knew every twist and turn of these paths, in the same way that I knew the ruts and potholes of the track to Stonegate and the wobbly steps of the spiral staircase in the lighthouse.

We passed the turning that would have taken us down to the harbour and instead we kept going, climbing the path that led up to the south cliff. The army had started to build something up on these cliffs. There was a tall barbed-wire fence and, beyond it, several half-built concrete structures. Amongst the bare wilderness of the clifftops, the wire and the concrete were so ugly, so out of place. The half-built shapes looked eerie in the mist – squat and sinister, like crouching toads. There was nothing else up here at all, just windswept gorse bushes and frost-bitten grass. The fog was thinner up here, and Mutti's shape became clearer. As she walked, ribbons of mist swirled around her feet like snakes. *Why is she going up here?*

I thought about that cryptic accusation from Kipper Briggs – *She's been seen.* Had he been talking about Mutti? What *was* she doing out on the south cliff in the darkness and fog?

The light was changing now – the black dissolving into a rusty grey. *The sun must be rising.* But there was a light ahead of us too – a pale, yellowy glow – then it was gone again, like a door or a curtain opening and closing. And then I remembered. There *was* something else up on the south cliff: Spooky Joe's cottage.

Spooky Joe had moved into the crumbling little house at the beginning of the previous summer. Everyone had assumed he was renting the cottage for a holiday, but months later he was still there.

I'd never actually seen him – he kept himself to himself and was rarely seen in the village. Pa had told us about him – said that his name was Joe and that Mags and I should 'leave him well alone', so naturally this made us all the more intrigued, and we started making up stories about him being a smuggler or a murderer or a spy. I can't remember which of us came up with the nickname Spooky Joe, but it seemed to have stuck.

Whenever we walked up this way, we always kept an eye out for him, but he was never more than a shadow at the window, a puff of smoke from the chimney, or a pair of black boots disappearing through the doorway.

When Mutti was about fifty yards away from the cottage, she stopped quite suddenly and ducked behind a gorse bush. It was then that I realized we were not alone on the clifftop. There was another figure too, just ahead of Mutti. It was a wraithlike shape, distant in the mist. Then the bizarrely comical truth of the situation became clear.

I had been following Mutti, but she had been following someone else.

8

I didn't ask Mutti what she was doing that foggy morning, and I didn't ask her who she had been following. I couldn't find the right words without sounding as though I was accusing her of something terrible. And I couldn't admit that *I* had followed *her*. We had always been such a close family, we had always trusted each other, but secrets had started to seep into the gaps between us. And now, like water freezing in the cracked surface of a stone, those secrets were growing colder, harder, starting to force us apart.

The very next morning, Pa and Mutti sat us both down at the kitchen table and told us that we needed to have 'a serious conversation'.

My stomach cramped with guilt — *Am I in trouble?* I always feel like that when a grown-up says they need to talk to me about something serious. It happened a lot at school: the headmistress, Mrs Baron, could make me feel quite sick with one of her penetrating stares. It was usually Mags who was in trouble, not me, but I'll bet Mags has never had a guilt-cramp in her life.

'We've been reading about the programme for evacuation,' Pa said, putting his hands down flat on the table.

'Evacuation?' I looked from him to Mutti.

Mags wasn't looking at either of them; her eyes were fixed on the window, and the cold, grey, drizzly world outside our cosy kitchen.

'Yes,' Mutti said. 'Children are being sent away from their homes to different parts of the country – to places that are safer.'

'We know all about it,' I said. 'Mrs Baron told us at school. We've even got two new children from London in our class. They came a couple of months ago.'

'That's right, Pet,' Pa said. 'Right now, the government say that the Kent coast is considered to be safe. But it's possible that this area too may need to be evacuated in time, and we wanted to discuss it with you first. The government have already evacuated children from London and other big cities . . .'

'But this isn't exactly a big city, *is it*?' Mags interrupted, her eyes still fixed on the window.

'Let me finish, please, Magda,' Pa said calmly. 'And they will need to evacuate children from *anywhere* that becomes a target for attack. If things change, we need to know that the two of you can be moved quickly to a safe place inland.'

Inland. Even the word made me feel panicky and claustrophobic. It's a feeling that might be difficult for you to understand, unless, like me, you've grown up by the sea. I can't bear the thought of being boxed in by buildings, shut away from our enormous skies and the clean salt-washed air and all the colours of the sea.

'If the princesses are staying put, I'm sure it will be fine for us to stay too,' Mags said airily. We had heard something on the wireless about the royal family deciding to keep Princess Elizabeth and Princess Margaret at home rather than send them away to Scotland or Canada. Trust Mags to remember that.

'Magda,' Pa said in one of his strictest voices. 'Firstly – though this may be hard for you to believe – you are not actually a princess. Secondly, you haven't even thought about it properly yet. Don't fly off the handle so quickly. This could be a chance for you to visit a beautiful part of the country, like Devon or Cornwall – lots of evacuees are going there – down in the southwest.' He took a pencil from his top pocket and sketched out a rough map of the country on the front cover of yesterday's newspaper. I watched the shape growing on the page, corralling all those words about the war within its familiar borders.

I love maps. It is, I think, quite natural to love maps

when you grow up in a lighthouse. I got a gold star in the first geography lesson I ever had at school: I found the work so easy, so natural, because the maps and the smooth-rolling surface of the globe made perfect sense to me. It was the world seen from above – the blue of the sea, the green of the land, the jigsaw-edges of the coastline: the whole world looking exactly as it does from the top of our lighthouse.

As Pa's map of Britain took shape, he told us about Dartmoor and Exmoor and wild ponies and golden beaches with rocky coves. I tucked my knees up on the kitchen chair and stretched my jumper down over them. I gazed out of the window into the drizzle, thinking about galloping across different clifftops, exploring new rock pools and caves. I imagined watching the sun setting over the sea instead of rising from it.

'Will the other children in the village be going too?' Mags said. 'I mean, will everyone be going?'

'We don't know yet,' Pa said. 'But if our coast becomes dangerous, it would certainly be the most sensible thing.'

'What would happen to our school?' I asked.

'Well, in most cases so far, the school teachers have accompanied the evacuees. I think normal school would probably be closed for a while . . .'

I couldn't help grinning at this – *No school!* Mags indulged me by pulling a silly, excited face.

Pa shook his head at us.

'Girls, this is *very* important,' Mutti said, '*Please!*'

My insides lurched as I realized that my mother was trying not to cry.

'Sorry, Mutti,' I mumbled. She looked so fragile all of a sudden. Pa put his hand on her shoulder.

'I just . . . I really do think we need to be prepared,' she said. 'I couldn't bear to be parted from you both, but . . .' She trailed off, and her eyes settled on Mags. 'It's not just about the risk of attack, my darling, is it?' We looked at her, waiting for the other reasons, but none came. She twisted her hands together, took a long, trembling breath and turned towards the window. Did she know something we didn't know? I wondered if it could have had anything to do with her sneaking out of the cottage so early in the morning – following a mysterious figure across the misty clifftops. *Something has happened that has made her think we will be safer if we leave Stonegate.*

'You think we should go, don't you, Mutti?' I said.

She nodded, and so did Pa. That made me feel very odd indeed – both our parents saying that they wanted us to go and live somewhere else. I felt I was about to cry too, but I couldn't tell if it was because I was feeling sorry for myself, or if it was because Mutti was so upset.

'But we wouldn't know the people we were staying with, would we?' Mags said then. 'They could be anyone at all, couldn't they?'

'Well – someone with a spare bedroom who wanted to help others. You will find that most people are kind, Mags,' Mutti said, blotting the tears from her eyes with Pa's handkerchief.

'And what happens when they discover that we are half-German, Mutti? Do you think most people will still be kind to us then?'

There was a leaden silence. My chest tightened. We looked at Mutti, and Mutti looked at Pa, fresh tears welling up in her eyes.

They had not considered this.

The logs in the kitchen stove crackled. The drizzle outside thickened, running down the kitchen window in thin grey worms of water.

PART TWO

Spring 1940

9

So we weren't evacuated, and nor were any of the other children from our village. Not yet, at any rate. The early months of the war slid quietly by. Christmas and New Year came and went. The blossoms of spring had just started to fade when Hitler invaded France, and the war truly began. Terrible things started to happen one after the other then, with the dreadful, unstoppable momentum of storm waves at sea.

We listened to the wireless every night, and every night it was clear that the German army was getting closer and closer to our little island: sweeping through the Netherlands and Belgium; surging up through France. It is difficult to describe what we all felt, but I can tell you that my Wyrm nightmare tormented me every single night – a monster crawling from the water and clawing its way up the cliffs to the Castle. A monster from which I knew there could be no escape.

After the eeriness of the Twilight War, the darkness was now upon us at last. People continued to go about their everyday business, of course – weeding the garden and sweeping the step, and their words were defiant . . . But everyone was afraid. They were afraid that we would be next.

At about six o'clock one morning, I sat up in bed, suddenly and completely awake. Something was wrong. *Smoke.*

The smell of a burning building is unmistakable; even my dozing, dreaming brain knew that this was not a smell from the kitchen stove or the sitting-room hearth or even a bonfire. I leapt out of bed, yelling to Mags, and ran through the cottage from end to end, expecting to see flames at any moment. I burst through the kitchen door and stared up at the lighthouse too. But there was no fire to be seen.

Then I heard Mutti's voice behind me – she was up and dressed already: 'The village, Petra – it's all right, my darling – it's coming from the village.' She put her arm around me. 'Over here – look . . .'

We went towards the cliff path and I saw it straight away: a cloud of dirty grey smoke. It sat over the village below, bulging and billowing. The breeze pulled at the smoke, tearing off woolly skeins of it and carrying them up towards us.

'What is it?' I asked. 'What's on fire?'

'The village hall,' Mutti said, 'according to the postman.'

I tried to make out the shapes of the familiar buildings, but everything was obscured by the smoke. The bell of a fire engine echoed over the fields.

Mags and I dressed quickly and ran down to the village, but by the time we got there the fire was almost completely extinguished. A crowd had gathered in the street. Some people were still wearing slippers and dressing gowns. They frowned and folded their arms and shook their heads and muttered to each other.

The smoke was dispersing already, but the firemen were still pumping water on to the walls of the village hall and the nearby church tower, to prevent the fire from rekindling and spreading. On the opposite side of the road, all that remained of the Scout hut was a pile of charred metal struts and some blackened sheets of corrugated iron. It had been little more than a large shed, tucked between the school house and some old cottages, and now there was nothing left of it. Mags and I sidled around the crowd to get a better look. The stench of smoke was fierce here, and I knew Mutti would insist on washing our hair this evening, whether we liked it or not.

I looked at the two buildings – from one side of the

street to the other. It didn't make any sense. 'How could the fire have spread?' Mags muttered. 'The buildings aren't even touching – they're on opposite sides of the road.'

I nodded.

One of the firemen was rummaging around under the bushes beside the remains of the Scout hut, right next to where my sister and I were standing. He found something – a large tin, and he used a stick to pull it out of the nettles. He passed it to the senior fireman standing next to the engine. They spoke quietly, but we were just close enough to hear.

'Paraffin?'

He sniffed at the can. 'Petrol, I think. Could make it easier to trace, seeing as it's being rationed so strictly now.'

The captain nodded in agreement. 'It's what we thought, then. And I've just been told it was being used as a base for the Local Defence Volunteers. We need to inform the police.'

The Local Defence Volunteers? Pa had just signed up. There had been an announcement on the wireless – all able-bodied men aged seventeen to sixty-five who were too young or too old to fight, or were in the reserved professions, were asked to volunteer for the LDV to help defend the country in the event of an invasion. Just this week the village hall had been agreed upon as the base for meeting and training, and the

Scout hut had been secured for storing equipment. And then, only a few days later, both buildings had been set on fire.

Mags and I left the crowd at the village hall and walked towards the shops. Mutti had said she would meet us outside the butchers.

After we had been walking quietly for a moment, Mags said, 'So it was deliberate, then? Someone set the village hall and the Scout hut on fire deliberately? With petrol?'

'It looks like that,' I said.

'But why? And why target the LDV? Pa said they haven't even got properly started yet. He was getting all cross about it – do you remember?'

I did. Pa had been talking to Mutti last night. He had said the volunteers were so frustrated with the lack of proper equipment that a plan was being cooked up by the local farmers to arm the LDV with their own collection of rabbit rifles and shotguns. They were taking matters into their own hands.

'Maybe it's got nothing to do with the LDV or the war. Maybe it was a personal vendetta.' I said. 'Or an act of passion.'

Mags rolled her eyes at me. 'An act of passion, Pet? In Stonegate Scout hut? I very much doubt it.'

Then we saw Mutti waiting there for us outside the butcher's shop. She was looking at Magda with a peculiar, worried expression on her face. When we got closer, she shook the expression away and handed my sister the ration book.

'See if you can get some bacon, please, Mags,' Mutti said, with a quick smile. 'Pet, let's go and see Mrs Rossi at the bakery.'

'Flames as high as the church tower,' one woman said. 'We thought it was the end of days!' There was quite a queue at the bakery, and everyone was talking about the fire.

'Was it children, do you think?' said another. 'I heard some of the lads got their hands on a recipe for a sort of homemade bomb that you can make in lemonade bottles. If Jerry shows up, they're planning on chucking them at him!'

'If Jerry shows up,' someone else echoed, 'I'll be chucking more than flamin' lemonade bottles – I'll chuck the kitchen sink'n'all!'

People laughed. But then there was another voice from the front of the queue, low and cold: 'The thing is, ladies, Jerry's *already here – isn't she?*'

It was an old man I didn't recognize, and he had turned around to stare straight at my mother. There was a terrible silence. I looked at Mutti. What was she going to say?

But Mutti didn't say anything at all. She looked at me, and then looked down so no one could see the tears that had already started in her eyes. Someone giggled. Someone else shuffled her feet, and then whispered in her friend's ear. My face was burning. Perhaps I should say something – *Don't talk about my mother like that, you nasty old man!*

But then Mrs Rossi said very briskly, 'Thank you, sir. Who's next, please, ladies?' and the dreadful silence eased.

When we got to the front of the queue, Mrs Rossi leant across the counter to Mutti and whispered, 'Don't pay any attention to him, my dear.'

Mutti nodded. Her eyes were very sad. 'He lost his brother in the Great War, I believe.'

She knew this horrible man? But I had never seen him before in my life.

'Ah.' Mrs Rossi seemed to understand. 'He finds it hard to be kind, then, I think,' Mrs Rossi said. 'Hard to forgive.'

'Yes. It is very difficult for him.'

'Difficult for you too,' Mrs Rossi said, her chocolate-brown eyes looking at Mutti with sympathy. She and her husband were from Italy – she knew what it was to feel like an outsider in a village like ours. I saw her slip an extra bun into our paper bag. 'Difficult for all of us, my dear.'

IO

The fire wasn't the only act of sabotage. Just a few days later, three telephone lines in the village were cut, including the line to the police station. At first it was blamed on high winds, but when the man came to repair them, he said it was obvious the lines had been severed deliberately. It was starting to become clear that there was someone in the village who was not on the same side as everyone else. People looked at each other differently when they passed in the street, searching each familiar face for a trace of something sinister. *Is it you?* they seemed to say, as their eyes narrowed with suspicion; they hugged their shopping bags tightly as if someone were about to make a grab for them. And all the time that fishing net full of Smith family secrets kept squirming heavily in my mind, and the unspoken mistrust between us grew deeper and more dangerous.

Sometimes, I felt I barely knew my sister any more. Despite food rationing, she was shooting up and suddenly seemed about a foot taller than me. She had started to pin her hair up on her head, using the curls to conceal her sticking-out ears. Then, one day, she announced that she was dropping out of school.

'It just feels *ridiculous*,' she said to Pa, 'copying out of dusty old history books when history is happening all around me right now and I could be doing something practical to help.'

'You're still too young for the Wrens, Magda,' Pa replied.

'But I could volunteer. I could volunteer on the lifeboat until I'm old enough for the Navy.'

Mutti looked at Pa as if she were trying to tell him something with her eyes. Her expression was grim, but she didn't say anything.

Pa sighed. 'I'll talk to the boys at the lifeboat station tomorrow.'

Mags looked delighted. 'We'll go together?'

'We'll go together.'

I remember that next day very well. Mags was up earlier than usual, and washed and dressed before any of the rest of us. By eight o'clock she was waiting for

Pa in the kitchen.

And at nine o'clock she was still waiting.

At half past nine she gave up. 'Where *is* he?' she said to no one in particular.

'I don't know, darling,' Mutti tried to soothe her. 'He went out for a walk early this morning – perhaps he got held up somewhere, or stopped off at the farm or the village . . .'

'Or perhaps he just forgot,' Mags interrupted. And she went straight to our bedroom and slammed the door.

At almost exactly the same moment, the kitchen door flew open and Pa appeared, holding what looked like a box of goodies from the grocers.

'Who wants a breakfast picnic?' he said, a broad smile plastered across his face.

He might as well have said we were off to have tea with a mermaid. 'A breakfast picnic? There's no such thing, is there?'

'There is now,' smiled Pa. 'We've got fresh bread and butter, scotch eggs, sausage rolls straight from the oven, oranges, and I'm going to make us a big flask of hot cocoa too.'

I gasped. Pa must have decimated the ration book.

'My darling, what's the special occasion?' Mutti asked, standing up and giving him a big kiss on the cheek.

'Do we need a special occasion?'

Mutti smiled and kissed him again. It was like the sun coming out after weeks of rain – I had forgotten what their faces looked like when they were lit up like that. For months now they had both been so pale and pinched with worry.

It was my favourite sort of weather – breezy and cool but gloriously bright. We made for the sunny, seaward side of the lighthouse, and Mutti spread blankets out on the rabbit-nibbled grass. Mags followed a few minutes later. I had managed to entice her from the bedroom by reciting a list of all the wonderful food we were about to devour without her, so she tagged along, but I could tell that she was still upset with Pa.

We tucked into the sausage rolls and hot cocoa straight away. It didn't take too long for Mags to defrost – after all those mornings of margarine scraped over a thin slice of wheatmeal toast, who could have resisted a breakfast banquet like this?

'I haven't forgotten about the lifeboat station, Mags,' Pa said to her quietly, when he didn't think anyone was listening. 'We'll go tomorrow. All right?'

'All right,' Mags said after a moment, giving Pa one of her sideways smiles. Then she shoved an entire scotch egg into her mouth, and I thought I was going to die laughing.

I will always remember that morning. I couldn't have known it at the time, but it would become the last, truly happy memory I have of all four of us together. It was as if the tensions and distrust of the past few months had been washed away, and we were as we'd been before the war began. How I wish someone had taken a photograph of us – Pa with his arm around Mutti's shoulders, Mags spraying crumbs everywhere as she laughed, the Daughters of Stone standing like sentinels around our little family and, above us all, the enormous spring sky, as blue as a balloon and bursting with promise for the summer ahead.

But then again, I don't really need a photograph, do I? I can see it all perfectly whenever I want. I just have to close my eyes.

'Tell us the story, Frederick,' Mutti said.

'The story of the Wyrm and the Stones?'

'Yes.'

So he did. We gathered close, and Pa told us about the fog and the fishermen, and the four daughters who sang to the sea, promising the greatest of sacrifices if it would only bring their fathers safely home. When he got to the bit about the Wyrm spitting out the boat and devouring the souls of the daughters instead, I couldn't help shuddering – just as I had when I was four years old.

My eyes were drawn towards the sea. There was no sign of a German U-boat – in fact, there had been no more sightings since the day of the crabbing competition – but the Wyrm was there, as it always was. Its long, serpentine shape quivered hungrily beneath the waves. The Daughters seemed to be looking at the water with me, staring down at their cruel enemy, never letting the Wyrm out of their sight. The stones versus the sea-dragon. The Wyrm may have petrified the Daughters for thousands of years, but in that moment I had an oddly certain feeling that the battle was not yet over.

When we returned to the cottage, the grocery box was empty and our tummies were full. Mags led the way, carrying the blankets, then came Pa and Mutti with the empty box and bags. I brought up the rear (determined to get the last few drops out of the cocoa flask).

'Really, Frederick,' Mutti said, 'that was so lovely, but for the rest of the week we will be living off vegetable soup!'

'I know,' he replied, with a strange little laugh. 'But it was such a beautiful morning . . .'

'It's the war,' she said, and they both stopped walking. 'So much darkness. It makes you want to hold every bright moment.'

'Yes.' He pulled her close to him and kissed her on the forehead, closing his eyes very tightly. 'It's the war, my darling.'

Then Mags called back over her shoulder, 'Tomorrow, Pa. You promise?'

Pa held Mutti close for a moment longer, then he swiftly wiped his cheek with the back of his hand. He took a quick breath.

'Yes. Tomorrow, Mags. I promise.'

But the next day brought something else entirely.

II

The sound of the anti-aircraft guns ripped through my dreams, splitting the silence of the dawn – an impossibly loud CRACK CRACK CRACK.

I heard Mags fling herself out of bed and run straight to the window.

I stayed exactly where I was. I clamped the pillow around my head and lay perfectly still under the blankets, curled up like a hedgehog, my breathing quick and shallow.

'There's a plane!' Mags shouted. 'A German plane! It's—'

And then came the explosion. It was much more than just a sudden, deafening boom – it was a sensation too. It was as if the explosion happened inside my chest, inside my head. Everything buzzed with the force of the blast, everything was shaken to its core. There was a high-pitched ringing in my ears now, and Mutti was shouting, 'GIRLS! HERE! GAS MASKS!'

But there was no need for the gas masks as it turned out – there was no gas, and there had been no bomb.

'It's CRASHED!' Mags bellowed. 'The plane just crashed into Mr White's cabbage field! Our guns must have hit it!'

It wasn't long before a crowd from the village came up the cliff path to have a good look at the German aircraft that now lay crumpled and smouldering amongst the cabbages. Mags and I went too, pulling on wellies and coats over our pyjamas. Pa was already there, helping Mr White, the farmer, to cordon off the wreckage to discourage children from looking for 'souvenirs'.

'As if we'd be that silly,' I said.

Then I saw Michael Baron pick up a fragment of metal half-buried in the ground beside his boot. He wrapped it in a handkerchief and stashed it in his pocket.

Kipper Briggs and his father were there too. Kipper and Michael eyed each other from a distance like tomcats. Kipper said something to his father, and Mr Briggs's response was to cuff his son casually around the head. Kipper slunk away but Mr Briggs stood there in the mud for a minute or two longer, staring at the huge, blackened skeleton of the plane. He shook his head, looking even angrier than usual.

Mrs Baron was wearing her spotless ARP warden's uniform.

'She got that on pretty quickly,' Mags hissed irreverently. 'Perhaps she wears it to bed, just in case.'

I snorted and gave my sister an appreciative shove. For a moment, she was the old Mags again.

'Clear the area, please!' Mrs Baron was shouting, using what I recognized instantly as her Headmistress Voice. A few people shuffled about between the cabbages, in order to look as if they were being cooperative.

'Well done, gentlemen,' she said to Pa and Mr White, gesturing towards the posts they had just hammered into the earth. She smiled at them and Mr White nodded and touched his cap. Then she lowered her voice: 'I take it there were no . . . survivors?'

Mr White shook his head gravely. 'Not a chance, ma'am,' he said. Then he picked up his tools and set off towards the farmhouse while Mrs Baron attempted to shepherd the crowd.

Mags and I managed to duck behind her, so she didn't see us inching towards the cordon. The plane lay face down in a mess of chalky soil, shards of metal and blackened cabbages. Flames still played about the charred fuselage and dark spectres of smoke rose into the air. The smell of burning was acrid, brutal. A gaggle of children from the village were jumping about, cheering. I turned my back to them.

How many men were inside? I wondered. *How many lives plummeting towards the ground, knowing that these were their final seconds?*

'I need everyone to leave the area,' Mrs Baron shouted. 'Clear the area, please! *It is not safe!*'

As we followed Pa back towards the lighthouse, I felt a flush of pride that it was my Pa who had got there first and had known what to do. He wasn't just one of the gawping crowd; he had done something useful. In that moment, I felt very important and very special.

Mutti had not wanted to come and see the crashed plane. She stood at the gate, her arms wrapped around her middle, waiting for us to come home.

I waved at her, then looked up at the sky, and took a long lungful of the morning. It had rained heavily overnight, and the air was filled with the scent of fresh rain, damp earth and the churning sea. The blustery wind was already carrying away the bitter smell of the smoke and the burnt cabbages, and the sun was trying to break through the clouds. Two or three narrow shafts of sunlight streamed down, spotlighting patches of the swollen ocean and our Castle — a brave silhouette against the silvery sky.

Then Mags interrupted my thoughts. 'Who's that?'

she asked. She was looking beyond the lighthouse, towards the south cliff. A man was standing on the ridge, staring down at us. The wind was whipping my hair around, so I held it out of my eyes, squinting up at the figure. I couldn't make out his face, only the squarish set of his shoulders and some rather wild, white hair.

'I can't see his face properly, but it might be that man who was so rude to Mutti in the bakery. Could he be one of the fishermen?'

Mags shrugged, frowning. 'I've never seen him before,' she said.

Mutti must have noticed the direction of our gaze, as she turned to look behind her. Pa looked up too then, and stopped walking. There was a very odd moment when all four of us were looking up at this mysterious man, and he was looking steadily back at us. Time seemed to hold its breath. The wind dropped. Pa raised his hand in a sort of wave, but the old man turned his back and walked away.

I couldn't have explained it at the time, but I was somehow aware of the significance of this moment. A shiver scuttled down my spine.

12

I asked Mutti about the mysterious old man when the two of us were up in the lantern room later that day. We were both drawing, as we often did. I looked and looked at the view, then closed my eyes, folding up the sea and the stones and the sky into my mind. Then I opened my eyes again, picked up my pencil, and tried to unfold it all on to the paper. But the sea was all wrong, and the sky had no depth, and the standing stones were just flat, childish shapes.

I sighed and put my pencil down. 'But if you don't know who he is, why did Pa wave at him?'

Mutti said nothing. She was sketching a cloud, shading and shading its full, grey shape until it looked as if it were about to burst with rain.

'And wasn't he the man who was so horrible to you

in the bakery? You said he had lost his brother in the Great War. You knew him.'

'*Please*, Pet,' Mutti said. 'Can we talk about this another time? I have so much on my mind today.' Her fingers tightened on the pencil and the cloud grew darker.

Barnaby the cat prowled into the lantern room then – the lion of our lighthouse. He trotted towards me, leapt on to my lap and patted my pencil with a huge fluffy paw. Then he sniffed at my sketchbook, and lay down on it, his big soft belly eclipsing my scribble. I sighed and gave up.

Mutti looked at me, then turned back to her rain-cloud. 'Everything has a song, Pet,' she said. 'If you listen carefully to the song of something as you are drawing, it will help you to capture its soul.'

I listened, trying to let go of all my questions for Mutti's sake, trying to hear the song of the sea. *The sea has many different songs*, I thought. There are days when its song could be played upon a harp, but on this day it would have been something much more solemn: a slowly-bowed cello, perhaps. The water was like mercury – heavy and quivering.

I was starting to understand what Mutti meant, but I still couldn't draw it.

Then there was a high, whistling noise from the speaking tube, and Mutti leapt up. Barnaby leapt up too, digging his claws into my legs as he flew from my lap and disappeared down the stairs. My sketchbook and pencil clattered to the floor.

The speaking tube is a long hose that goes between the lantern room and the kitchen below. Mutti removed the whistle from the brass end of the tube, and put it to her mouth. 'I'm here,' she said. 'Is there any news? Has it arrived?'

It must have been Pa, down in the kitchen. We usually used the speaking tube to tell Pa that dinner was ready, or he might use it to ask us to bring him up a cup of tea. This conversation sounded a lot more serious.

'When?' Mutti asked, and pressed the brass piece to her ear once more. The long, white hose wriggled and shook in her hand.

'But that's so soon,' she said, and she sank back into her chair. 'That's the day after tomorrow.'

'What is, Mutti? What's the day after tomorrow?'

But she was listening to Pa. Eventually, she fixed the whistle back into the brass mouthpiece with shaking hands.

It took her a moment before she could say anything. 'I've been summoned to a tribunal, Pet,' she said at last.

'A what?'

'A sort of trial. I have to go to court.'

13

Because Mutti had been born in Germany she was officially an 'enemy alien', and every enemy alien in the country now had to be officially assessed and categorized according to the risk they represented to the security of Great Britain. The three categories were A, B and C.

Category A aliens were considered a serious threat and were to be locked up in internment camps; category Bs were not to be locked up, but they faced restrictions on where they could live and what they could do; category C aliens were not considered dangerous at all and were free to continue their lives as normal.

In the next village, there lived a nice old couple called Mr and Mrs Miller (they had changed their name from Müller to Miller when they moved to

England from Germany). Mr Miller was a writer and his wife was a musician. They had disagreed with a lot of the things that had started to happen in Germany and it had become too dangerous for them to stay there. They had decided to leave and start a new life somewhere else before it was too late. Their tribunal had taken place just a few days before and they had been classified as category C, so they were free to return to their home.

'There is nothing to worry about,' old Mr Miller said to Mutti, as the four of us stood on the sunny steps of Dover Magistrates' Court that morning. 'This is a good country – a free country. They will see the truth in you.' He smiled warmly, and so did Mrs Miller, her face crinkling up like tissue paper.

The three magistrates sat on what looked like wooden thrones, side by side behind a long table.

'Three Wise Monkeys,' whispered Mags. I shook my head at her, but she was spot on, as usual.

1. Sir Alan Darsdale, sitting on the left, deaf as a post and half-asleep in a dusty ray of sunshine, was Hear No Evil.

2. Mr Gibbons, in the middle, peering suspiciously at Mutti through his spectacles, was See No Evil. His eyeballs were inflated into ping-pong balls by the thick lenses.

3. Mrs Baron sat on the right. Her arms were folded and her lips were pressed together in a

benign and professional smile. For the time-being at least, she was Speak No Evil.

Mrs Baron began proceedings. 'Another straightfor-ward case, I'm sure we all agree,' she started.

Mutti turned her head towards Pa. He tried to smile at her, but she couldn't smile back. Her hands were white, twisted together tightly in her lap.

'Mrs Angela Smith—'

'Mrs Angela *Zimmermann* Smith,' Mr Gibbons corrected.

'Thank you,' Mrs Baron continued. 'Born in Munich but moved to England in 1922 when you were eight-een – is that right?'

'Yes.' Mutti nodded, standing up quickly. 'Your Honour.'

'And you came here because . . .?'

Mutti hesitated for a moment. 'I was supposed to go to Paris to study art, but my family's savings were no longer enough . . .'

'Ah, yes, we've all heard the stories – wheelbarrows of money just to buy a loaf of bread – that sort of thing?'

'Yes. So it was decided that I would come to England instead – to work. My mother's cousin ran a small hotel here – Mrs Fisher.'

'Of course – we all remember Mrs Fisher. The flowers in the village church haven't been the same since she passed away . . .'

There was an indignant 'Hmph!' from an old lady called Bertha Daley, sitting at the back. She had taken over floral responsibilities at the church just a few months ago.

'I met Frederick, and we married not long after.' Mutti smiled at Pa. I could feel him wanting to reach out and squeeze her hand. I wanted to as well.

'And you registered as a German national when you moved here?'

'Of course – as soon as I arrived.'

A pause while Mrs Baron checked the paperwork in front of her. 'Yes.'

A different voice now – it was Mr Gibbons: 'Do you still have family in Germany, Mrs Zimmermann Smith?' He squinted at her through his glasses.

'Both my parents have died,' Mutti said, her voice a little quieter.

'Eh?' shouted Sir Alan Darsdale.

'Both my parents are dead now,' Mutti said more loudly, her voice catching a little.

'Ah,' said Sir Alan Darsdale, and nodded, his eyelids starting to close once more.

'But there are . . . cousins, I think?' said Mrs Baron. She was looking at a piece of paper.

'One cousin. Max,' Mutti replied. 'But we are not in touch.'

I noticed that Pa gripped his knees so tightly his knuckles had gone white.

Mrs Baron pushed the piece of paper over to Sir Alan Darsdale, who snored at it. Mr Gibbons then read it, holding it up close to his face. He stared hard at Mutti and his ping-pong-ball eyes looked bigger than ever.

'Where does your cousin live?' he asked.

Mutti paused for a second – just a second. 'In Berlin,' she said, then added, 'I believe.' Someone behind me inhaled loudly and whispered something.

'And when was the last time you had contact with him?'

Mutti paused again. 'I have not seen him for many years,' she said at last.

'Really?'

'Yes,' Mutti said. 'Not for many years.'

Mrs Baron paused and then said, 'Is there anything else of which the court should be aware?'

'I don't think so . . .' Mutti began.

But then something happened.

'There *is* something else, I'm afraid,' said Mr Gibbons, and he held up a folder of papers. Sir Alan Darsdale jerked awake. This was most irregular. 'Apologies to my fellow magistrates for the lack of formal procedure,' said Mr Gibbons, 'but this only came to my attention immediately before the session.' He frowned a little and looked at someone sitting at the front of the court – a tall, thin man in a very smart pinstriped suit, who stretched his legs out in front of him and folded his arms across his chest. The man's face was craggy – the wrinkles and worry lines that marked his forehead were so deep they almost looked like scars. He cleared his throat – a dry little sound that sounded a bit like the cough of a fox – and he nodded, almost invisibly, to Mr Gibbons.

Mr Gibbons then whispered something to Mrs Baron and pulled the documents from the folder. He leafed through the pages, showing her one after another.

Mrs Baron grew very pale. Her hand moved towards her mouth.

The same documents were then shown to Sir Alan Darsdale, who said nothing but raised his bushy white eyebrows until they almost met the curls of his magistrate's wig.

Sir Alan Darsdale cleared his throat. 'The court will take a brief . . .' he announced loudly, then muttered, 'What's the wretched word?'

'The court will adjourn for a few minutes,' said Mrs Baron, and I noticed that her voice had changed.

Automatically, my hand reached for my sister's. She placed her other hand quickly over mine.

As soon as the three magistrates left through the rear door of the court, the room erupted with noise. I looked around. Everyone was chattering, their eyes alight with the melodrama of the moment. I thought perhaps I was going to be sick.

'Pa?' I said. But he was having a silent conversation with Mutti.

What's happening? her eyes said to his.

I don't know, I don't know, said his in reply.

I had never seen Mutti look so white and small. She suddenly looked terribly young, younger even than me. I noticed that a policeman who had been sitting in the front row had stood up and was now hovering a few feet behind her, watching her warily, as if she were a wild animal, or a bank robber with a gun.

14

When the magistrates came back into the courtroom, Mrs Baron's face looked very strange, as if it had been stitched up and the thread pulled too tight.

'I'm afraid we have a very difficult decision to make,' she said. 'The police in London have intercepted a package on its way to Germany. A package of information and drawings. There are records and charts on the movements of British Naval vessels, and drawings depicting Stonegate harbour, the port of Dover and surrounding shipping hazards such as the sandbank off Dragon Bay. What can you tell us about these drawings, Mrs Zimmermann Smith?'

'Drawings?' said Mutti. They were passed to her and she looked at them, shaking her head.

Mr Gibbons's full-moon eyes were fixed upon her: 'You said yourself that you were destined to study art in Paris. You told us that just now, or do you deny it? You *are* an artist, are you not? You draw?'

'I draw, yes,' she said. 'But these are not mine. I draw the sea, the cliffs, the storm clouds, the birds in the sky – these are . . .' She struggled to find the right word. 'These are more like *maps*, *diagrams*.'

Mr Gibbons shrugged. He did not see the difference.

Then a voice called out from the back of the court: 'Of course they're her drawings. She's always out on the cliffs with her flamin' pencils.' It was Arthur Briggs.

Mags held my hand more tightly.

'Order!' shouted Mrs Baron. 'If you have evidence, Mr Briggs – proper evidence – you had better stand up. If not, you must keep silent or you will be removed from the court room.'

There was a moment of silence. Mutti was staring towards the back of the court, her mouth slightly open. She was breathing quickly. Then Arthur Briggs got to his feet.

'All I'm sayin', Your Honours, is that I've seen her.' A few people nodded. Mags was facing forwards, quite stiff and still. She was holding my hand so hard it almost hurt.

'She's been creepin' about on the cliffs,' Briggs went on. 'I've seen her meself. There's new army buildings being built up that way, aren't there? Bunkers? Guns? Things Jerry would want to know about, I'm sure!' A murmur bubbled up from the benches at the back.

'Order!' shouted Mrs Baron again.

I remembered Kipper Briggs and his accusation: 'She's been seen.' I thought of that misty morning when I had followed Mutti up on to the south cliff. I knew she wasn't drawing diagrams of the harbour or the new army buildings – *of course* she wasn't – but . . . what *was* she doing there? Who had she been following? It didn't make any sense. I felt Mags shift in her seat beside me. Her hands, clasped around mine, suddenly felt clammy.

'And she lives in the *lighthouse*, for Pete's sake!' Briggs added. 'She's probably flashing secret messages to Fritz every flamin' night!'

Another murmur of noise.

'How do we know she wasn't to blame for the fire in the village?' someone else shouted. 'Or that bomber that our guns took down? She might be using the lighthouse to signal to the blimmin' Luftwaffe for all we know!'

People were muttering in agreement, heads nodding all around us now.

Who were these people?

I will tell you who these people were. They were our friends. People from church, the village shopkeepers and fishermen, the parents of the children we had grown up with. But something had changed them. The war. The enemy plane. The things they had heard on the wireless and read in the newspapers. The rumours, the whispers. They were angry. And they were very, very frightened.

'Thank you, Mr Briggs,' said Mrs Baron. 'You may sit down.' She looked at her fellow magistrates, and the two of them nodded at her gravely.

Then Pa stood up, and my heart leapt – he was going to defend Mutti. 'I wish to—' he started, but Mrs Baron did not want any more interruptions or surprises.

'I think we've heard *quite* enough from the court's spectators today, Mr Smith. I'm so sorry. Your loyal support of your wife is noted. You may sit down.'

Pa stayed standing, his mouth open. He seemed unsure of what to do.

'You can sit down,' she said again, looking into Pa's eyes. Her tone was firm. *Trust me*, she seemed to say.

When Pa eventually sat down, Mrs Baron took a deep breath. 'Mrs Zimmermann Smith,' she began, 'has shown herself to be a woman of excellent character, as *everyone* in the village knows.' This remark seemed to be directed towards the back of the courtroom. I looked up at Pa. *A woman of excellent character.* It was going to be all right, wasn't it?

'We are at war, though, and a huge responsibility rests upon our shoulders. We must . . .' She stopped. I had never seen Mrs Baron lost for words before. She looked at Mr Gibbons and he stood up.

'Ladies and gentlemen, these drawings are frankly rather frightening,' he said, addressing the courtroom as a whole. 'They suggest that someone in the area is indeed attempting to provide information to the enemy for the purposes of strategic advantage, attack and possibly even invasion.'

Several people gasped.

'We cannot at present prove Mrs Zimmermann Smith's guilt in this respect, and, indeed, we are not here today for a criminal prosecution of any sort – that responsibility will lie in other hands.' His eyes flicked briefly towards the man in the pinstripe suit sitting in the front row. 'I am afraid, however, that there is sufficient evidence to suggest that Mrs Zimmermann Smith might be a potential threat to national security, and we can't ignore that risk. We are under very strict instructions.'

Mags gripped my hand tighter. We were both rigid – made of stone. Tears were running down my face. *They can't . . .*

'Category A,' Gibbons announced.

A triumphant release of breath from the back row.

'Eh?' said Sir Alan Darsdale.

'CATEGORY A.'

Excited muttering all around me.

'Mrs Angela Helene Zimmermann Smith, you are

to be indefinitely interned as a matter of national security . . .'

Everything was blurred now – the faces in front of me, the white wigs and wooden thrones, the sound of Mr Gibbons's voice, the words themselves . . . *Interned. Indefinitely interned. Imprisoned. Taken away. My Mutti.*

'Pa?' I grabbed his sleeve, but he was just staring at Mutti. His lips were moving silently, as if he were trying to say something.

Mutti stood up, but the policeman had to help her. He took her by the elbow and led her out of the court-room. Her eyes did not leave Pa's until she was forced to turn at last through the dark doorway.

On the steps of the court outside, the sun was shining as brightly as it had before, but now it felt all wrong. Everything felt all wrong. Four of us had gone into the court, but only three of us had come out. I had that horrible, incomplete feeling you get when you know you have forgotten something very important. I felt sick.

Pa was in the middle of us, holding our hands – Magda's and mine – and we descended the steps slowly, looking down. We did not want to talk to the chattering crowd that waited for us.

Mrs Baron was there on the steps too. 'I'm so sorry,' she said, 'I'm so sorry, girls, but our hands were absolutely *tied*.' She hugged Mags, and then she hugged me too. But I didn't want hugs from Mrs Baron; I wanted my Mutti. I was so frightened I could hardly breathe. For some reason, all I could think of was the grip of the gas mask, the choking bitterness, the suffocation . . .

15

After the tribunal, the police came to the lighthouse. Mutti had to wait in the police car while the officers collected some personal belongings that she could take with her to the internment camp, but she wasn't allowed in, and we weren't allowed to go out and talk to her. I stood in the kitchen staring out at the police car. Mutti was just a silhouette in the rear window — so far away from us. I felt all buzzy and strange, as if I were lost in a bad dream.

Mags was sitting on a kitchen chair, drumming on the table with her fingers. The drumming grew louder and louder, faster and faster. Eventually she stood up, shoving her chair back so hard it fell on the floor with a crash. Then she strode out of the door, slamming it back against the cottage wall. A policeman was standing by the car and she was walking right towards him.

Pa called out, 'Magda – WAIT!' But she ignored him.

I remembered the fight she had got into on the first day of the war. My sister was a force to be reckoned with. *What is she going to do?* I wondered. *Push the policeman off the cliff? Rip open the door of the police car and rescue Mutti?* In that moment, striding forward, with her mess of brown curls streaming out behind her, my big sister looked ten feet tall, like some sort of warrior queen. I had complete and utter faith that she was about to save the day.

But she didn't push the policeman or even go near the police car; she turned towards the ridge. Then she broke into a run, and stumbled up the path towards the south cliff.

She's gone. She's left me. I blinked a few times and shook my head, as if trying to wake up.

Pa came back inside and the two policemen came in after him.

'Mind if we have a quick look around while we're here?' they asked Pa. He nodded helplessly and sank down on to a kitchen chair, his face slack with shock.

The thin man in the pinstriped suit sidled through the kitchen door too. Where had he come from? He must have been sitting in the back of the police car with Mutti, but I hadn't noticed him. He didn't say anything at all, just nodded politely at us and wandered around, his hands clasped behind his back. He had a very odd way of looking at things, as if he were memorizing every detail.

On the door that led into the snug were pinned a collection of drawings and paintings that Mags and I had done when we were little, and the pinstriped policeman stopped to look at them now. He leant in closely to examine six-year-old Mags's 'ship sinking in a strom', and then studied my 'JIANT SEAMONSTER IN AUTUM SUNSET'.

I stared at the familiar, brightly coloured shape that was bursting out of the blue waves – a misshapen head full of triangle teeth. *This war is a sea monster*, I thought. *Sometimes it destroys things violently and openly, and sometimes its tentacles squeeze in through the cracks of normal life, and it strangles us silently.*

The policeman touched one of the pictures, and his mouth twitched as if he were trying not to smile. *Perhaps he is kind*, I thought, but then he did the dry little fox-cough that I remembered from the courtroom, and asked if one of us could show him up to the lighthouse. Kind or not, he was looking for evidence – something that would prove my Mutti's guilt. My heart stuttered in my chest.

Pa couldn't say anything – he looked as if he could barely move. So it was down to me.

'Watch the first step,' I said as my trembling hands unbolted the metal door at the foot of the staircase.

'It's a bit wonky.'

We climbed the spiral stairs, through the service room, all the way up to the lantern room at the top. As we climbed, my mind was racing ahead, trying to remember all the things that were usually lying around up there. *Could there be anything that would make them think Mutti was a spy?* I led the way, so I could pause for a moment at the top of the narrow stairs, feigning breathlessness and blocking the pinstriped man's view of the room.

I could see drawings, pencils, binoculars . . . *Oh, God . . .*

'I won't keep you long,' Pinstripe said, and pushed gently past me into the lantern room. 'Oh, I say – what a view!' He stood there, awestruck for a second (as most people do when they step into our lantern room for the first time). 'We're up in the clouds!'

I could hear the heavy boots of the two other police-men thumping up the stairs behind me. I didn't have time to hide anything.

'What exactly are you looking for, sir?' I managed to say, aware of a familiar numbness spreading up from my toes . . . I knew that feeling: I was starting to freeze.

Pinstripe didn't reply, but the first policeman did. He almost fell upon the binoculars as he lurched into the lantern room: 'These'll do for a start,' he said, examining the binoculars very suspiciously. He put them into a special bag he took from his pocket, handling them with care. *Not a very pleasant-looking chap*, I thought: he had an oily moustache that drooped across his top lip like a damp bootlace.

'We'll have to check them for fingerprints,' he whispered to his colleague with an air of self-importance.

The numbness was spreading up my legs now, through my hips and – with a surge of nausea – through my tummy too. My fingers clung stiffly on to the handrail at the top of the stairs. Mags wasn't here to be my fierce big sister. Pa was downstairs, in pieces. I had to be braver. *Petra Zimmermann Smith*, I said to myself, *You are the only one who can help Mutti right now.*

'Of course they'll have my mother's fingerprints on them,' I managed to say, my words catching slightly in my throat. 'They'll have all our fingerprints on them – they're *our* binoculars!'

'Oh, yes?' said the second policeman, noticing me properly for the first time. '*Your binoculars*. And what exactly do you all look at through these, then?'

I rolled my eyes at the policeman's ignorance.

'Birds, mainly,' I said, 'or the moon, or boats . . .' My throat closed up. Was looking at boats too incriminating?

He narrowed his eyes at me.

Behind the policemen was a pile of Mutti's drawings. Would they class those as evidence? Probably. I would have to distract them.

'You should check the doorknobs for Mutti's finger-prints too,' I said, swallowing hard and trying to ignore the tremor in my voice. 'And you should probably check her toothbrush while you're at it.'

Pinstripe made a little noise then that might have been a suppressed laugh. He was examining the speaking tube with interest. I forced another breath in through my tightening throat. As long as he was looking at the speaking tube, he wasn't looking at the drawings.

'That tube goes down to the kitchen so you can talk to whoever is in there and ask them to bring you up a sandwich or something.' I was beginning to gabble now. As I spoke, my eyes flashed over to the pile of sketches. They were on a seat just a few paces away. The policemen still hadn't seen them. 'You talk into the tube and then put it to your ear to listen to the reply,' I went on. 'That brass piece is a whistle. If you attach it, people at the other end can get your attention by blowing into the tube and sounding the whistle.' I don't know why I was telling him so much. Once I had started, I couldn't really stop. But there was also something about the way Pinstripe listened – tilting his head slightly to one side like a robin – that made me keep going. 'Mags and I used to use it to eavesdrop on whoever was talking in the kitchen, until Mutti told us it was bad manners. If you listen very carefully, you can usually pick up the conversation, even if people aren't speaking directly into the tube.' Pinstripe raised his eyebrows. He put the speaking tube to one ear.

'All quiet in the kitchen now,' he said softly.

I pictured Pa, all alone, pale and sunken in his chair.

'Is it possible,' hissed the first policeman, 'that the suspect could have used this device for listening in on Mr Smith's conversations with the Admiralty?' He slicked down his oily moustache with a finger and looked very pleased with himself.

There was a pause. The second policeman nodded, impressed, and started to write something down in a notebook he fished out of his pocket.

'No,' I said, as firmly as I could manage. 'The telephone is in the service room on the floor below.' Then, to make them feel even more stupid: 'You walked right past it on your way up the stairs.'

The oily policeman smiled at me – a sarcastic, fleeting little smile. His moustache twitched. He put on a pair of gloves, and started turning the pages of Pa's logbook – the official record of lighthouse activity and various weather and shipping charts. He showed it to Pinstripe. The second policeman was poking around in a cupboard full of tools and oil cans.

It was now or never. I tried to move my feet, but they felt as if they were made of solid ice and I could barely shuffle forward an inch. My hands were cold and sweaty on the handrail, and my heart was beating so rapidly against my ribs that it felt like a moth inside a jam jar. I stared at the pile of drawings, willing myself to move closer to them, but panic had turned me to stone and there was nothing I could do. My breath came more and more quickly and the room started to spin, the spiral stairway became the centre of a whirlpool. I blinked, gripping the handrail tighter. *Come on, Petra*, I said to myself. *You need to be better than this — you need to be braver.*

'Are you all right, miss?' asked Pinstripe, coming over. He looked at me closely, as if I were another item in the room to be inspected. 'Perhaps you could go down to the kitchen, Constable? Bring up a glass of water.'

'Yes, sir.' The second policeman nodded and went down the stairs.

I couldn't help myself. My gaze darted over to Mutti's drawings again — and Pinstripe saw. He walked over, picked them up and looked through them slowly, one at a time. I held my breath. There was one drawing he stopped on for some time — a skein of wild geese flying over the lighthouse.

'What's that you've got there, sir?' the moustached policeman asked. He was still flicking through Pa's logbook.

'Oh, nothing important.'

Pinstripe came back over to me and handed me the drawings without a word. I tucked them behind my back.

'Come along, Sergeant,' Pinstripe said. 'Nothing more up here. Let's have a look in the office – and bring that old logbook, will you? Just in case it's useful.' And the two of them went down the stairs.

My eyes closed. Just for a moment, it felt like a triumph, but then there was the sound of the police car starting up outside. I moved at last, my feet full of pins and needles but obedient once more. I walked to the window that looked inland, and I watched the police car take my Mutti away. I watched it until it was a dot on the distant hillside.

And then it disappeared.

16

The weather that night was fierce. I remember the wind howling around the lighthouse, ripping at the long grass on the clifftops and whipping up the wildest waves I had ever seen. The sea surged in huge black breakers, exploding in ice-white spray half a mile high. Each one of those waves could have swallowed a ship.

Sitting by the fire in the cottage, we turned off the wireless and just listened to the wind as it screamed through the cracks in the window frames. Mags sat in Mutti's armchair and stared into the fireplace, hypnotized by the hell-red glow of the last burning log. It smouldered angrily, and so did my sister. She had been out all afternoon and had barely said anything since she'd got back. I still hadn't forgiven her for leaving me to face the policemen alone.

Pa looked up, and we heard a tile grate and clatter its way down the sloping roof. 'It was a storm to raise the dead,' he whispered to himself, as if he were remembering the beginning of an old ghost story.

The thing is, on our bit of coastline, storms actually *do* raise the dead. There are hundreds of wrecked ships buried within the Wyrm. Hundreds of them. Every now and then – once or twice in a lifetime, perhaps – a heavy storm churns up the ocean floor, causing the sandbank to shift and convulse so that it spits out a rusty trawler, or the rotten corpse of a lost sailing ship. Sometimes they stay drifting there for a few days and can be recovered, but more often than not, the sandbank sucks them back down again – hoarding its grim trophies beneath the waves.

At the very lowest tide, you can see what looks like a forest of dead trees sticking up out of the shallow water. But they are not trees at all – they are the masts of ships long buried in the sandbank. They are skeletons in a watery graveyard. The remains of the Wyrm's prey.

As I tried to sleep that night, I thought about my Mutti, spending her first night away from us, locked up in an internment camp. I wondered if the storm was keeping her awake too. I remembered the German lullaby she used to sing to us when we were little and couldn't sleep – the one about the moon rising – *Der*

Mond ist aufgegangen. I sang it silently in my head and tried not to cry. I didn't want Mags to know how frightened I was.

Sleeping was like falling into a series of shallow black holes; I woke over and over again, yanked up into consciousness by the wind tearing at the tiles on the roof, or the blast of waves pounding into the cliff face below my bed. When I was awake, I thought about the faces of the people who had turned against Mutti in the courtroom – people who needed her to be the enemy so that they could do something with all that anger and fear and hate they had inside. I thought about the Nazis creeping closer and closer to us through the darkness; I thought about a U-boat hanging there in the murky-green gloom, far below the churning surface of the Channel. All through that long, stormy, miserable night, visions of the Wyrm writhed wildly in my mind.

'Are you all right, Pet? *Pet?*'

My sister's voice. Her hand on my shoulder, shaking me awake.

It's not real, then – the sea-dragon squeezing and scraping its way up the lighthouse steps, the hiss of its rotten-fish breath, hungry jaws filled with row after row of teeth . . . I don't have to hide any more – it's not coming for me. It's not real . . .

'Pet!'

'Uh?' My breathing was quick, dizzy. My pillow felt

wet under my cheek.

'I think you were having that nightmare, Pet. That one you used to have when you were little. You were sort of . . .'

'I was what?'

'Whimpering.'

I sat up in bed. Our room was still dark, the ugly blackout curtains drawn tightly together. 'Is it morning?'

'It's early. Five o'clock, I think.'

'Did I wake you?'

'I was awake anyway.'

I squinted at the dim outline of my sister. 'Are you dressed, Mags?' She didn't appear to be wearing her usual striped pyjamas.

'Yes. I'm going out. I've had an idea.'

'What?'

'If Mutti didn't do those drawings,' she whispered, 'then someone else did. And if we can find out who the real spy is, we'll be able to prove Mutti is innocent. Come with me, Pet.'

I sat there in the darkness. The last of the storm was over us now, and rain spattered rhythmically on the window.

'Right now?' My nightmare had left me shaken and frightened – I didn't think I'd be able to move.

But Mags was not afraid at all. 'Come on, Petra,' she said. 'For Mutti.'

*

The rain was easing as we set off, pulling on dark-coloured clothes and tucking our hair up into old woolly hats. Mags wore her satchel. She had packed a torch, an emergency jam sandwich, Pa's brass telescope (as the police had the binoculars), and a notebook and pencil to write down the exact details of everything we saw. What we really needed was a camera, but we didn't have one. We crept out of the house without turning any lights on and closed the door softly, so we wouldn't wake Pa.

In the spring, our clifftop used to be bright with blossoming gorse, the new grass nibbled by a hundred baby rabbits, but now it was a grey, thorny wilderness of metal and concrete. The government had reinforced the coastline with trenches, barbed wire, pillbox guard posts. Perhaps this should have made me feel safer, but instead it reminded me of how close the enemy really was – a bit like when you're playing tag and you slam the door behind you and shove a chair up against it. The wind had dropped and it was eerily quiet outside. As we made our way up the dark, wet path to the south cliff, my imagination conjured the sound of enemy boats landing on the beach below us, the crunch of enemy boots on the sand.

'Where are we going, Mags?'

'Not far. Not far at all now . . .'

Spooky Joe's cottage loomed ahead of us – a low,

dark, square shape. From a distance, it could almost have been one of the pillbox concrete bunkers. I was reminded of that misty morning a few months before when I had followed Mutti up on to the south cliff.

'Quiet now,' Mags hissed. 'We don't want him to know we're here.'

Her plan suddenly became clear.

'Spooky Joe?' I breathed. 'You think *he's* the spy?'

Mags nodded. 'Think about it, Pet,' she whispered as we left the path and tiptoed behind the cottage. The blackout blinds were still down. 'He moved here just before the beginning of the war. He's got this amazing view out over the Channel – it must be nearly as good as our view from the Castle. *And* he's virtually a recluse – no one really knows anything about him.'

I considered her arguments. They certainly seemed to make more sense than Mutti being the spy.

Mags and I took up our positions behind a gorse bush.

'What are we going to do, Mags?' I whispered.

'I'm not sure yet,' she replied, taking the bag off her shoulders and rummaging inside for Pa's telescope. 'Let's just see if he . . .'

And then there was a noise from the cottage. A grating sound, like a bolt being drawn back.

'He's there!' Mags squeaked, pulling me down into a crouch beside her. 'It's Spooky Joe – he's coming out!'

17

She was right. From between the gorse thorns, I could just make out the door of the cottage opening, and then a figure appeared. A squarish figure in a long, dark coat. The clifftop breeze whipped at his white hair and he turned up his collar. I had seen this man before.

'Do you remember, Mags? On the day the German bomber crashed – he was standing there on the ridge watching the whole thing. Staring at us.'

'Yes,' Mags breathed. 'Yes! That was him. That was Spooky Joe . . .'

'He's the old man who was so horrid to Mutti in the bakery. He called her Jerry.'

My sister's eyes narrowed. 'What's he doing?'

Spooky Joe was doing something very peculiar. He

edged his way around the side of the cottage nearest us and lowered himself down so that he was lying on his front in the grass. Then he wriggled inland and uphill. From the top of that rise he could see all the way down to the Dover Road – the view was almost as good as from the lighthouse. He rolled on to his side and pulled some things from his coat pocket. He put a pair of binoculars to his eyes. Then he appeared to write or draw something on a piece of paper.

Mags looked at me triumphantly. 'I knew it, Pet!' she whispered. 'I knew he was the spy!'

'But he's facing inland,' I hissed. 'What on earth is he looking at?'

'I don't know. Stonegate church? The telephone box? I need to see what he's writing down . . .'

We kept watching. Spooky Joe squinted through the binoculars again and continued to scribble for a minute, then he crawled back down the hill, pushed himself up and went into the cottage, leaving the paper weighed down by the binoculars.

'I'm going to go and have a look,' said Mags.

'Are you mad?' I whispered. 'He's probably just gone in to get something. He'll come back at any moment! Mags!'

But she was already running across the grass.

My eyes flicked back and forth between the door of the cottage and my insane sister. My heart was drumming fast and my breathing was changing. *Oh, God, not now* . . . I could feel the dreaded pins-and-needles feeling starting in my fingertips.

Mags was nearly at the top of the rise, trying to keep low but moving as quickly as possible. Just as she reached the piece of paper on the grass, there was a tapping noise behind her and she spun around. A loud grating sound followed, and a bang – a window being flung open – and then a voice: 'HEY!'

Mags stared for a second, then grabbed the piece of paper and started running back towards me at full pelt. But she didn't reach the gorse bush. At the last moment, she swerved and made for the cliff path instead. Perhaps she thought it would be quicker to sprint down to the village that way. But Spooky Joe wasn't chasing her – he came through the door of the cottage, and then he stopped. There was a skidding sound just a few yards away from me – shoes on loose stone – and a scream. *Mags!*

My limbs had gone all weak and watery and I was panting for breath – I couldn't stand up properly. I managed to crawl a little to the other side of the gorse bush. Mags had run straight into a coil of barbed wire and was trying to disentangle herself, looking around desperately and pulling at the barbs with bleeding fingers.

Then there was a voice: 'Well, fancy seeing you up here, Miss Smith. Bright and early, as usual.' It wasn't an old man's voice, it was boyish and cheerful – a voice full of ease and charm. Michael Baron.

'Looks like you could do with a bit of help,' he said. He knelt down beside her and examined the tangle of wire and fabric. 'Don't,' he said, stopping her from grabbing at the wire. 'Don't, Magda – you'll hurt yourself.' My sister twisted around again, still frightened of being pursued by Spooky Joe, but he had gone. The door of the cottage was shut.

'It's all right,' Michael said soothingly, 'I've got just the thing.' He reached into a pocket and pulled out some sort of tool or penknife. He clipped at the wires one by one, carefully disentangling them from Mags's clothes.

'Thank you, Michael,' she said, a little calmer now. I noticed that the piece of paper had gone from her hand – she must have put it in her pocket. She looked down at him.

Michael grinned up at her. 'A Boy Scout is always prepared, Miss Smith,' he said with a wink. 'Not that I'm a Boy Scout any more . . .'

Mags laughed. I had never heard her laugh like that.

He stood up then. 'Hang on,' he said, his voice a bit softer. 'What's this?' He reached towards her face and gently untangled a bit of dead gorse from a strand of hair that had escaped from beneath her hat.

Mags's eyes were locked on his and her face flushed pink. 'Thank you, Michael.'

'My pleasure, Miss Smith. Anything to help a damson in distress.'

'A damsel,' she corrected.

'No. More like a damson,' he said, and touched her blushing cheek. I watched my sister's face turn an even darker shade of pink.

'I'm just up here for a walk with my sister . . .'

'Oh, yes?' He looked around. It must have been a bit odd that he couldn't see me. I stood up on trembling legs and waved at him from behind my gorse bush. He waved back at me, looking only slightly puzzled. 'Are you going down to work on your boat this morning?' he asked my sister.

She hesitated, tucking her ears firmly beneath her woolly hat. Then she smiled and said, 'Yes. You can come too if you like, Michael.'

So they set off together and I tagged along behind, glancing back over my shoulder every now and then to make sure Spooky Joe wasn't following us. What had he been up to? It had certainly looked like spying of some sort, but what could he have been looking at? And what was written on the piece of paper Mags had taken? I wanted Michael Baron to go away so that we could have a look and discuss it properly, but as I watched them walking along together, side by side, it became clear that any conversation with my sister was going to have to wait until later.

18

'We'll take the tunnel,' Mags announced, and my heart sank. She knew how much I hated the shortcut down to the beach. Was she trying to shake me off – hoping I'd leave her alone with handsome Michael Baron?

Something flared up inside me. I wasn't going to be shoved aside. Besides, if I turned around to go back home via the cliff path, I would have to go past Spooky Joe's cottage, alone . . .

'Are you coming, Pet?'

I smiled as innocently as a younger sister can at moments like this. 'Of course,' I said.

The entrance to the tunnel was concealed by the ruins of an old lookout tower and the roots of a gnarled, wind-bent tree that grew from between the stones. Most of the children in the village knew about the tunnel. It was a secret passed amongst siblings and school friends, though our Pa had been the one to show it to me and Mags. It was a long, steep, enclosed passageway carved through earth and chalk and tree roots – an old smugglers' route that took you from the south cliff all the way down to the beach at Dragon Bay.

We used Pa's torch, its feeble beam illuminating the chalky burrow just a few yards ahead. Michael went first, then Mags, then me. Here at the very top, the tunnel was the entrance to an enormous rabbit warren and, as we dropped down on to all fours, we had to watch where we put our hands, as there were little piles of droppings here and there. Something blinked in the gloom, and scurried away down a narrow hole with a flash of feet and a blaze of tail.

I hated this first bit. Tree roots cobwebbed the walls of the tunnel and dangled down into our path. Sometimes they were sturdy enough to be helpful – you could grip them and lower yourself around the steep, twisting corners; sometimes the thicker roots blocked the way, hanging there like pale stalactites, and you had to hold your breath as you squeezed between them. They were rough and scaly, and caught on my woolly hat and hair. The passage was so low that, in places, we had to wriggle on our backs or bellies. My left foot caught in a root and, for a second, I couldn't budge. As Michael and Mags got further ahead, the light of the torch died out completely, plunging me into darkness.

'Mags!' I called. 'I'm stuck.'

'Just wriggle your way through, Pet — pretend you're a mole or something.'

I forced my foot back, hearing the root tear behind me. Some loose soil pattered down from the ceiling of the tunnel. I forced in a deep breath of the damp, earthy air and struggled on, following my sister's squirming feet. I felt myself getting angry with her, exactly as I had in the rowing boat on the day of the crabbing competition. Why did I let her get me into scrapes like this?

As we got deeper inside the cliff, the tunnel became steeper. The walls here were chalky — pale and smooth as old bones. There were parts that were almost high enough to stand up in, with steps carved into the chalk, and lower stretches where we had to tuck down on our haunches and skid and slither our way down into the darkness. I felt my boot scrape against some-thing sharp and the same thing tore at my coat. I thought about how angry Mutti would be when we got home and she saw the state of my clothes — and then I remembered that Mutti wasn't at home any more. Tears started burning in my eyes and I had to bite my lip. Then, dim morning light illuminated the tunnel ahead, and the passageway twisted around a tight corner, suddenly opening up into a much larger space.

Here, halfway down the cliff face, was a round cavern with two window-like openings that looked out over the sea. This was Dragon Bay Cave. It must have been a perfect lookout spot for the smugglers who had first used the tunnel all those years ago, as they could have watched the boats making their way around the dangerous coastline, flashing signals to them with lanterns held up at the round, chalky windows.

Michael stood at the right-hand window now. 'Such a fantastic view,' he was saying. Then, more quietly: 'I love being here with you, Magda.'

I was confused. Had they been here together before, then?

Mags's face was shining, but I felt as I always felt when I stood here in the cave. I felt *eerie*. The two windows at the front made me feel as if I were inside a giant skull, peering out through the hollow eye sockets.

'Just look at the Wyrm,' I muttered, staring out through the left eyehole. I looked down, and swallowed.

The tide was coming in, the sands were shifting, and the yellow-grey Wyrm was twisting about hungrily beneath the shallow waves.

'It must be tricky, that sandbank,' Michael said. 'If you're manoeuvring a big ship, or a submarine or something like that.'

'It's fine if you know what you're doing,' Mags said with confidence. This was her favourite subject. 'And the lighthouse gives you the perfect bearing to steer safely around it into Dragon Bay or Stonegate harbour.' She looked at Michael. 'I can show you if you like.'

He nodded, keen as mustard. 'That would be wonderful.'

Down at Dragon Bay, Mags led us straight to the line of upturned rowing boats that were pulled up high on to the dry sand, out of reach of the tide.

'Aren't we going to take the motor boat?' I asked. Pa had salvaged the rusty old wreck from the scrapyard as a project for Mags. When we first got it, it just about managed to stay afloat, but the engine had needed rebuilding. Mags had christened her *Faith*, and she was moored in the harbour.

'No, I haven't quite got the engine running yet,' Mags replied.

'But you've been working on her for *months*, haven't you?'

I might have been mistaken, but I thought Mags flashed a look at Michael then.

'Of course I have. But there's so much that needs doing before she's safe and seaworthy. Come on – we'll take *Edward*.'

Edward, or rather *King Edward*, was the family rowing boat we had used for the crabbing competition

– a lovely old thing, painted red, blue and white. I used to think it was odd that we had a boat named after a potato, but it had been Pa's since he was a boy (when King Edward VII was on the throne). Pa had passed it on to Mags, who had always tended it lovingly. If Mags went missing on a summer's day, she could usually be found down here on the beach, sanding, repairing and repainting *King Edward*, her sleeves rolled up to her elbows, flecks of paint in her messy hair. My sister had always smelt of yacht varnish and the sea.

Michael and I helped turn the rowing boat over, and then we dragged it down towards the water. There were long lines of barbed wire all along the beach, scoring the sand like razor-hooked fishing lines, but someone from the village had flattened sections of it, and cut other parts back so that children could still take their little boats out or swim in the bay. It was probably against the law, but no one seemed to mind much and the coastguard had turned a blind eye.

When we got to the water, Mags turned to me and said, 'Why don't you wait here for us, Pet? The boat isn't really big enough for three. You could do some drawing or something.'

I stared at her, and she stared steadily back. Her clear, dark eyes said, *You're not welcome.*

There were lots of things I could have said to my sister at that moment, but the one that came out of my mouth was, 'I can't draw – I haven't got my sketchbook.'

'There's paper and a pencil in my bag,' she laughed, tossing me the canvas backpack. Then she took off her coat, rolled it up, and threw it at me too.

I watched as my sister climbed into the rowing boat. Michael pushed the boat out until it was floating freely, then he climbed in too, and Mags started pulling at the oars. As the boat grew smaller and smaller, I became aware of my boots sinking more deeply into the sludgy sand, and the deeper they sank, the angrier I felt.

Mags and I had always squabbled, but usually Mutti forced us to make up quickly. 'Be the bigger person, Petra,' she'd whisper. It was always me that had to be the bigger person (even though I was much smaller). It was always me that had to apologize, to swallow my pride and say sorry. But then it wasn't possible for my sister to swallow *her* pride, was it? She had so much of it she'd probably choke . . .

I felt the wet sand closing over the toes of my boots. I turned my back on the sea, pulled my feet up with a revolting sucking sound, and returned to the higher, drier part of the bay.

I had been waiting for about half an hour, watching the quiet traffic of fishing boats on the glassy sea, before I realized that there was something very important that I could have been doing with my time. I could have kicked myself for forgetting about it.

I rummaged in the pockets of my sister's coat, and

found what I was looking for straight away. It was the piece of paper that Mags had taken from Spooky Joe.

I unfolded it, my heart pattering with excitement. *This could be the key to proving that Mutti is innocent.* I was expecting to find some sort of diagram, like the ones mentioned in the magistrates' court, but instead I found an incomprehensible list of numbers. This is what Joe had written:

MB – TB:
0617 040540
0638 110540
0557 180540
0625 250540

Was it a code of some kind? It was so unlike the documents at the tribunal . . . Perhaps Spooky Joe wasn't the spy after all. As much as I wanted this easy answer, it just didn't fit. If Joe was on the side of the Nazis, why had he made that comment about 'Jerry' in the bakery? No – Spooky Joe was a patriot. Perhaps he was keeping an eye out for suspicious behaviour, just like the government's posters told us to. Perhaps this note was the clue to who the real spy was . . . I couldn't make head nor tail of the numbers, but the letters at the top must mean *something* . . . What could MB stand for? The first thing I thought of was the person who was currently swanning about in the *King Edward* with my stupid sister – Michael Baron – but I knew that was nonsense. *It's just your anger talking, Pet*, I said to myself firmly. *Anyway — you're not really angry with him, you're angry with Magda.* And then I stopped and looked at the letters again. MB. Magda's middle name was Bernadette. Could Spooky Joe have been making notes about my sister?

I sat quite still for a moment. The salt-heavy breeze tugged at the paper between my fingers and a series of waves rose up and rolled in, one after another on to the beach. My mind churned like mud in the shallows. What if it *was* Mags? What if Mags had been up to something these last few months? I thought about her odd moods and behaviour, her early morning disappearances, the fact that she had obviously not been working on the motor boat, as she had claimed. She had been lying to us. And then I thought about that anonymous figure in the mist — could that have been my sister? Perhaps Mutti had thought Mags was up to something too. That was why she followed her that morning. That was why she was so desperate for us both to be evacuated . . .

I stood up, stuffing the piece of paper hurriedly into my own coat pocket as I realized that the boat sliding up on to the beach was the *King Edward*.

They were back.

19

On the way home, Mags turned out her coat pockets looking for Spooky Joe's note. 'It must be here *somewhere*,' she muttered.

'Perhaps it fell out,' I said, aware that my voice sounded stone-cold, and I didn't know if it was because I was so angry with her, or if it was because I was lying. 'It probably fell out as we were going down the tunnel.' *And you didn't notice*, I wanted to add, *because you were so bewitched by Michael blooming Baron.* My hand closed guiltily around the paper in my pocket, crushing it into a ball.

It was a strange, silent walk back up to the Castle. I couldn't bring myself to say anything to Mags at all, and, for the rest of the day, I could barely even look her in the face. Anger, doubt and suspicion were billowing in my mind like storm clouds.

When I came down to breakfast the next morning, there was a letter from Mutti waiting on the kitchen table. Pa must have just opened it, and was staring at it as if it had bitten him.

'Can I read it?' I asked.

Pa took a breath, and then nodded. 'Of course, Pet – it's to all of us.'

'I'll read it out loud,' Mags said, appearing from behind me and snatching it out of my hand. I hated it when she did her Big Sister act. On top of everything else that had happened recently, it made me feel like giving her an almighty shove, but Pa looked upset enough already, so I just shot her one of my foulest looks and went to sit at the other end of the table.

I tried to push all the terrible thoughts to one side and listened.

'*Dearest Fred, Mags and Pet,*

'*My darlings, I have been told that once a week I may write to you. I have been given this paper and told that I might write, but I am not allowed to write very much, so I shall (from now) try not to waste any words! I am well. It is quite comfortable here and clean enough, and the food is not too bad, but I am missing eating our home-grown vegetables. There are lots of people here who are kind and someone even shared a piece of chocolate with me yesterday. I have met a lady who is from Munich, near where I grew up. It has been very pleasant to speak in German for the first time in so long.*

'*There is a police inspector investigating the diagrams they showed me in court. He has been here to see me. He is a very nice man, and also clever. He may come to see you all at the Castle, so please do be helpful, but remember that I have told him everything he needs to know.*'

At this point, Mags's brow furrowed. 'What does that mean?'

She looked down again and read on.

'*Magda, don't forget to return or renew your Motor Boat Maintenance book at the library before the end of the month, or you will get fined again. Pet, I borrowed an umbrella from Mrs Rossi at the bakery when I got caught in that rain storm. For me, please could you take it back to her? Please take good care of yourselves, girls, and be as sensible as you can. Remember, even though I am not there to tell you, that I love you both very much and I will always be proud of you. Make sure you are doing everything you can to help your father.*

'*Fred, my darling, don't work too hard. Give Barnaby a tickle from me and tell him to leave the baby rabbits alone.*

'*I love and miss you all very much. Your Mutti xxxx P.S. Remember—*'

Mags turned the page over but there was nothing written on the other side. 'Remember what?' she said.

Pa stared for a moment, his eyes were open very wide. 'Perhaps she reached her limit of words,' he said. 'Or it might have been censored by the guards at the camp. Her letters will be checked before they are sent. It might have said something they didn't want her to say.'

'Like what?' I said, bewildered. 'It just sounds like she's going to remind us to keep our room tidy or feed the cat or something.'

'I don't know, Petra,' Pa snapped, taking the letter back from Magda. Then, straight away: 'I'm sorry, girls. I don't know.' He got up and put his jacket on. 'If anyone needs me, I'll be in the lighthouse.'

I took Mrs Rossi's umbrella back when I went down to Stonegate on Monday morning. There was no school now as arrangements were being made to send all the children in our area to a safer part of the country. Except us. Pa had decided that Mags and I would stay at home with him after all.

No school! A few months ago, I would have skipped all the way down the cliff path to the village, but I wasn't that girl any more. I walked quickly and stiffly, my hand clamped around the handle of Mrs Rossi's umbrella, and I recited Pa's shopping list in my head. He had entrusted me with the ration book and had asked me to collect some fish, a newspaper and a few other groceries. It was an overcast day and the air was very cool and damp. Rain started to fall – gently at first and then more steadily. I couldn't decide whether or not it would be wrong to actually use

Mrs Rossi's umbrella when I was in the process of returning it; handing it back to her all damp and dripping would be bad manners, wouldn't it? But then, with a darkening of the sky above, the rain doubled into a downpour, and I concluded that Mrs Rossi wouldn't mind at all.

The sea looked vast that day – as flat and grey as wet slate. It was calm in the way it often is in that sort of rain – patted down by the raindrops, flattened by the weight of clouds above. I heard the sound of an engine droning high in the sky above. *One of ours*, I said to myself, though I couldn't see the shape of the plane. *It's probably one of ours.*

I had become so used to the sounds of aircraft roaring back and forth above the Castle that it was difficult to remember a time when the cliffs were truly peaceful. I tried to keep the old cliffs in my heart, and I had Mutti's drawings and paintings to remind me of what it all used to look like before the bunkers and barbed wire. But that peaceful, safe, serene feeling was really hard to summon up now that the war was everywhere. Everything was different.

It was like being freezing cold – so cold your whole body is shivering and your teeth are chattering. When you're that cold, it is hard to imagine ever being too warm. Or like being so achingly hungry that you can't remember what it feels like to eat too much; such a sensation is impossible, surely? Well, that's what war does – it makes everything so different, so extreme, that you forget what life was like before. That first pang of hunger – the first hammering of the guns – comes as a shock. But then it all becomes normal.

20

It felt as if everything was against me — even the weather. As I made my way down to Stonegate, the cold rain ran down my legs and soaked through my socks and shoes. I hadn't stopped thinking about my mother's letter. In the light of my new suspicions about Mags, Mutti's words about loving us, and asking us to be sensible felt strangely weighted. Did she believe that Mags was up to something? Could my sister really be the spy? Was that why Mags had been so keen to shift attention on to Spooky Joe? The disloyal thoughts hit me swiftly, one after another, like punches in the stomach. I had never felt so adrift, so alone. And the only person I wanted to talk to about all of this was the only person I *couldn't* talk to.

When you share a room with a sibling, storms in

teacups are never just storms – they are tempests. Every little quarrel is more cruel and more intense than it would be otherwise, and this was something much more serious than a quarrel. When I thought about going to bed that night, I was filled with dread – I could already feel that cold, electric tension, crackling in the silence between our two beds.

Thunder. I turned my head sharply towards the sea as a booming noise quivered over the grey water. It boomed again – a terrible blast of sound. *Sometimes thunder sounds like an explosion in the sky*, I thought, but that was usually when a storm was right overhead, and there hadn't been any lightning yet. I walked more quickly, scampering down the path. If there was going to be lightning, I didn't want to be the idiot standing out on the clifftop holding a big umbrella.

The high street was deserted. Everyone else was being sensible – sheltering from the storm inside their nice, cosy houses. *I'll just get to the bakery*, I thought, *and perhaps Mrs Rossi will be kind enough to offer me a cup of tea and a biscuit while we wait for the rain to stop.*

But I didn't get that far.

As I was going past Mrs Baron's house, the glossy black door opened and a man came out. It must have startled me, I think, because I instinctively stopped and shrank back. Water from the gutter above splashed down on to my umbrella. I moved closer against the wall and watched as the door closed behind the man and he opened a black umbrella of his own. Then he clanked through the gate and set off down the high street towards the harbour. It was Pinstripe, the police detective. *Visiting Mrs Baron*, I thought, *to talk about the spying investigation*. They must have been discussing my Mutti.

I followed him. I didn't know if I had the courage to speak to him, or what on earth I would say if I did, but I had to find out what he knew.

I followed him all the way down to the harbour. The rain was drumming down on my umbrella, I wove around puddles and dodged wobbly cobblestones. Eventually, Pinstripe came to a halt at the harbour wall and I stopped too – a safe distance away, lurking behind a post box while I thought about the best way of phrasing what I wanted to say. The sky over the Channel thundered again.

'It's a terrible sound, isn't it?'

Was he talking to me? I waited behind the post box, not sure what to do. *He can't see me, can he?* I crouched a little.

'I can see your umbrella, Petra,' he laughed. 'It looks as if the post box is wearing a rain hat.'

Oh, Pet, you really are a first class idiot . . . I blushed as red as the treacherous post box, and stepped out.

'Sorry, sir,' I said. 'I wasn't spying on you or anything . . .' I faltered at my poor choice of words.

He smiled and was about to speak again when the sky boomed once more.

We both looked up at the heavy grey clouds. 'But there's no lightning,' I said.

'No,' he said. 'That's because it isn't thunder.'

I looked at him. *Not thunder?*

'It's guns.'

Guns.

'The German artillery.' He beckoned to me and I went to stand next to him at the harbour wall. He gestured towards the sea, towards France.

'Just over there,' he said, 'about twenty miles away, there is a little seaside town just like this one, with a beach and cafes and shops and things. And right now it is being bombed to bits by Hitler's guns.' His voice became quieter, and the creases on his forehead grew deeper. 'It's remarkable how close they are now. One is so much more aware of it down here.'

I stared out over the water, and swallowed. *A little seaside town just like this one . . .*

'Twenty miles isn't very far at all, is it?' I said, remembering some of the blisteringly long hikes Pa had taken us on over the years. 'For an army, I mean.'

Pinstripe shook his head. 'I came down from London on the train this morning, and that was about eighty miles,' he said. 'So, no. Twenty miles is not very far at all.'

We both looked out over the grey water.

'I need to tell you something, sir.'

He raised his eyebrows. 'Mm?'

'Mutti is innocent. My mother, I mean. It wasn't her who did those diagrams and things. It couldn't have been.'

He nodded, but his craggy brow was all bunched up. 'And how do you know that, Petra?'

My brain froze. *If you mention Spooky Joe's coded note, you could end up incriminating Mags instead of Mutti.*

Flustered, I said, 'She's just not *like* that. She might be German, but that doesn't mean she supports Hitler and all the terrible things he's doing. And she has nothing to do with any of the information that passes through the lighthouse about shipping or anything. If she were to look in Pa's logbook, I honestly don't think she would know what any of his notes or records meant.'

A little voice hissed in my head, *But Mags would — wouldn't she?* I swallowed hard, as if I could somehow get rid of the thought that way.

Pinstripe nodded. 'I see,' he said. He cleared his throat — that dry fox-cough. 'Well, thank you for that information.'

'Aren't you going to write it down? Doesn't it count as evidence — a character reference or something?'

Obligingly, he took a notebook out of a pocket and scribbled something down.

'She hasn't done anything wrong,' I said, determined to make him listen. 'And it's not fair that she should be locked up just because of the country she was born in.'

He didn't say anything.

I pressed on. 'She's a *good* person.' I was starting to get angry. The detective didn't seem to be listening to me at all; he was gazing out to sea again.

The rain became quieter, hardly falling now – just a damp thickness in the air. Pinstripe took down his umbrella, shook it and rolled it up. Then he looked at me. 'I'm sorry to say this, Petra, but sometimes, good people do bad things.'

I felt a stabbing pain in my chest. *Is he saying Mutti is guilty? That she is a traitor?*

'Why?' I said, fighting back the tears that burnt in my eyes. 'Why would a good person do bad things?'

He shrugged. 'The world is a complicated place and war is a terrible thing. Sometimes a good person has a logical reason for doing something that is morally wrong; sometimes they feel they have no choice.' He took a clean white handkerchief from his pinstriped pocket and offered it to me to wipe the tears away. 'I'm so sorry, but I'm afraid this is something you are going to need to come to terms with, Petra. Very soon.'

He knew something. He knew something that must prove Mutti's guilt, and he wasn't telling me.

All I wanted to do then – the *only* thing I wanted to

do – was to run straight home into the arms of my Mutti.

But she wasn't there.

I shook my head at the handkerchief, tightening my face and forcing a sob back into my throat. 'But you gave the drawings back.' I remembered how kind he had seemed in the lantern room – as if he were on my side. He hadn't let the police sergeant take Mutti's sketches.

'I didn't need them,' he said. 'I didn't need to take anything else.' Then again: 'I'm so sorry.'

He gave me a sad smile, turned away and walked back up the high street, through the dark, rushing streams of rainwater.

21

When I eventually got to the bakery, I was in a very bad state indeed. Mrs Rossi wasn't there, so I returned the umbrella to the shop girl, Edie, apologizing for its sogginess.

'Oh, I'm sure she won't mind, Petra,' Edie said nicely. 'It's what they're for after all, ain't it? A dry umbrella's a wasted one, eh?'

Edie talks too much and she's not exactly the brightest of sparks, but she's a very kind soul. She used to be good friends with Mags when they were at school together. Edie tucked a strawberry-blonde curl behind her ear, leant down and looked at me closely. 'You feeling all right, Petra?'

I must have wobbled a bit, as she got me a chair then and made me sit down.

'You look like death warmed up,' she said. 'Here . . .' She took an iced biscuit from the tray of baked goods under the counter. 'Don't tell anyone! You look like you haven't eaten all day. Honestly, this rationing'll be the end of all of us!'

I could hardly tell her what was really wrong, could I? That I was reeling from that terrible conversation – the booming of the German artillery, Pinstripe's words of doom . . .

'Yes, I'm probably just hungry.' I took the biscuit and nibbled at it. I inhaled the sweet, warm air. 'Thanks,' I said. 'I won't clutter up the shop for long, Edie. Pa's given me a shopping list and I'd better get to the fishmonger's before Arthur Briggs closes for lunch.'

'Well – I'm afraid you won't have any luck there,' Edie said.

'Why? What do you mean?'

'Fishmonger's been closed all day,' Edie said. 'Haven't you heard?'

'Heard what?'

'Arthur Briggs was arrested last night.'

'Arrested? What on earth did he do?' My head was full of spying and treachery . . .

Edie's curls bounced excitedly. 'Racketeering,' she said. 'Making a profit out of the war. He'd got his hands on a stash of forged ration coupons and was selling them off to his customers, apparently.'

'Good grief. Really?'

'Looks like he'll be in prison for a bit,' Edie said. 'Like your poor mum.'

I stared at her and swallowed a dry ball of half-chewed biscuit. 'My mum's not in prison, Edie,' I said.

'Oh.' She reddened slightly. 'Sorry, I didn't mean . . .'

'She's in an internment camp.'

'Oh. Right,' Edie said again. Then, after a pause: 'What's the difference?'

I thought for a second.

'Most of the people in internment camps are there because of who they are or what they believe, not for anything they've done,' I said. 'People go to prison for committing crimes.'

'Right,' she said again. 'I see. So your mum hasn't done anything?'

'No,' I said, 'other than be born in Germany.' Perhaps if I said it out loud it would help it to be true. I was ignoring the voice of Pinstripe in my head: *Sometimes, good people do bad things* . . .

'Well, that's a relief, then,' Edie said with a big smile. 'So she'll be coming home, then?'

I nodded, but when I tried to say *Yes*, my mouth wouldn't open.

There was a jingle and slam from the fishmonger's shop next door and, a second later, we saw Kipper Briggs skulk past the bakery window. He wore his black fisherman's hat pulled low over his brow, and the collar of his waterproof coat was turned up. His chin was tucked in against his chest, and his eyes were focused on the wet pavement beneath his feet. He looked smaller than he usually did – as if he had shrunk somehow.

'Kipper's very upset, of course,' Edie said.

'I'm sure he is,' I said, and was surprised at the pang of genuine sympathy I felt for him. I knew how terrible it was to see someone you loved being taken away from you. That tearing feeling in your chest. And the shame too – the police car, the gossiping crowds.

'He'll be taking on the family business now, I suppose. Reckon it'll be the making of him – a bit of responsibility, and that bullying dad of his out of the way. Under all that nonsense and bluster, Kipper's a good lad really.'

I thought about Kipper and wondered what sort of boy he would have been if he'd been lucky enough to have had a Pa like mine. Maybe it wasn't too late for him.

'Thank you so much, Edie,' I said, standing up at last. 'I feel better for that biscuit, but I'd better get on with the shopping. Pa will be wondering where his paper has got to.'

'Oh,' she said, 'I can save you the penny for the paper at least. Take this one, Pet – I've had a look already this morning and there's nothing in it to speak of.'

*

Pa was up in the lantern room when I got back. I put the groceries away and took the newspaper up to him, along with a cup of tea. The lantern room was filled with a strange, metallic light. It had started to rain again, and the grey skies filled every window, wrapped around us like a band of iron. *Should I say anything about seeing the police detective in the village?* It was probably better not to.

'I heard the German guns today,' I said instead.

Pa nodded grimly. 'Me too.'

I put his cup of tea down on a ledge and handed him the newspaper.

'Much appreciated, First Mate,' he said, and gave me one of his cheerful salutes, but it wasn't convincing.

'Edie at the bakery gave us the newspaper, so we've saved a penny there,' I said, passing him a handful of change. 'She said there's nothing much in it today anyway.'

Pa smiled a little. 'Did she, indeed? What – no half-price hat vouchers or free tickets to the pictures?' He shook the newspaper out and scanned the front page. Then his smile died completely.

'What is it, Pa?'

He didn't say anything. He swallowed and frowned, reading very intensely. The paper buckled beneath the grip of his fingers.

'Pa?'

I stepped around him, putting my hand on his shoulder. I tried to find the headline that had caught his attention. And saw it straight away.

TRAITORS TO BE HANGED
SWIFT PROSECUTION AND DEATH PENALTY FOR THOSE FOUND TO BE AIDING ENEMY — LORD BARTON COMMENTS ON NEW TREACHERY ACT

22

My nightmare about the Wyrm that night was worse than ever. I was in the water, swimming frantically, and the jaws of the sea dragon were right behind me. I dragged myself up on to the beach and it followed, squirming out of the sea. It somehow knew the way through the gaps in the barbed wire, and it clawed its way across the sand, up the cliff, into the cottage and up into the lantern room of the lighthouse where I was hiding. What was especially horrible about the dream this time was that I just gave up. I heard the hiss of its breath getting closer and closer, but I didn't try to run anywhere or fight: I just accepted that this was how my life would end – as a sacrifice in the foul jaws of the Wyrm. I was so frightened, so broken, that I was ready to welcome the darkness.

I woke up to the sound of arguing and the low burble of news on the wireless. The blackout blinds were down so I had no idea what time it was, and the horror of my dream still pulsed through me like poison. I lay still, trying to steady my breath.

'I'm going to go, Pa,' Mags shouted. 'You can't stop me!'

What was she shouting about? Go where?

'For the last time, Magda — I said NO.'

Were they talking about Mutti? Did Mags want to go and see her?

Yesterday's newspaper headline was branded in white-hot letters across my every thought. Pinstripe had suggested that Mutti was a spy, but that wasn't the only thing that now made me think she was guilty . . . There was something else too, something I had told no one else about.

Late last night, I had crept up into the service room to take another look at the newspaper article and, hidden away underneath it was the second page of Mutti's letter. Pa had hidden it from us deliberately, and as soon as I read it, I understood why. From her final words to us, it was clear that Mutti would be hanged as a traitor, and there was nothing any of us could do about it.

The missing page of the letter crackled softly beneath my pillow. My arms were wrapped tightly around myself beneath the blanket, but it didn't stop my hands and feet from trembling.

The voices in the kitchen rose up again: 'You can't possibly go over there by yourself, Magda – you'll be killed!'

'But thousands of our men will be killed unless we go and help them!'

They weren't talking about Mutti. What *were* they talking about? *Something to do with the war* . . . I got out of bed and went straight into the kitchen. It took a moment for Pa to notice me, standing there, pale and barefooted in my pyjamas.

'Nothing to worry about, Pet,' Pa said, though his face told me something very different. 'Your sister and I are having a discussion—'

'About *this,*' Mags interrupted, turning up the volume on the wireless. 'Listen.'

' . . . the Admiralty are putting out a call for all men with boating skills,' the announcer said. 'Especially those with a good knowledge of coastal navigation, who are capable of taking charge of a yacht or motor boat. Volunteers will be required to cross the Channel to Dunkirk in France to help evacuate British soldiers. All seaworthy vessels . . .'

'They're trapped,' Mags said, switching the wireless off. 'Thousands of our men are waiting there on the beaches right now – *thousands* of them! – cornered by Hitler's army.'

'Caught between the devil and the deep blue sea,' I said, still haunted by my dream of the Wyrm.

'Exactly,' Mags barked. 'And I can *help*.'

'*Other people* are going to help them, Mags, but not you. You're too young. And . . .'

'And *what*? And *I'm a girl*? Pa! You know I can man a boat better than most men in this village, better than most men in the *country*, I bet!' Her hair was wild, her eyes shone. There was nothing to be done with Mags when she had the wind in her sails like this.

Pa opened his mouth to say something, but no words came out. He held out his hands instead, as if begging her to *stop*.

'AGH!' Mags roared, exasperated. Then she flung the kitchen door open and stormed away. The wind slammed the door shut behind her.

Pa collapsed into a chair and closed his eyes.

I stood there for a moment, my feet freezing on the flagstones, just looking at my Pa. After seeing the newspaper headline yesterday, he had spent most of the afternoon and evening frantically polishing every bit of glass and metal in the lantern room, but he didn't whistle as he usually did when he did that sort of thing. After dinner, he had just sat there in his chair, exhausted, staring into space.

That was when I had gone up to the service room and found the hidden letter.

Pa sat in front of me now, his arms limp in his lap.

His eyes were still closed, but I knew he wasn't asleep. It was as if something that had been pulled tight inside him for months and months had finally snapped.

'Would you like a cup of tea, Pa?' I said.

He nodded, but his eyes remained shut.

23

Usually I would have left my sister alone for a while – she needed to cool down – but too much was at stake now. Too much had spiralled out of control already, sucked down into this terrible whirlpool. I had to try to forget about my suspicions, and all that stupid business with Michael Baron and Spooky Joe, and the note that was screwed up into a ball in the pocket of my coat. None of that mattered right now. Besides, how could Mags be the spy? Here she was, determined to sail across the Channel all on her own to rescue British soldiers. What sort of traitor would volunteer to do that? The only thing I really understood in that moment was the sickening fear that had wrapped its tentacles around me. My family was in terrible trouble, and if we didn't help each other, we would all be lost.

'Mags,' I said, when I found her, sitting behind the lighthouse amongst the standing stones. 'Please don't be angry with Pa – he's so worried about Mutti.' My sister was right by the edge of the cliff, plucking at a tuft of grass. I sat down next to her. 'He's so worried, Mags, I don't think he can bear to be worried about you too.'

'I know,' she said.

We sat there in silence for a while, and I sifted through the events of the past few days, trying to make sense of it all, but everything was too stirred up and muddied with fear. Mags held up her hand, letting some scraps of grass fall from her fingers. The wind blew them away from us, out over the cliff towards the cool, grey sea. Towards France.

A little seaside town just like this one . . . I thought about the German guns I had heard yesterday, and the radio announcement about the thousands of men trapped on the beaches. Just twenty miles away. I squinted at the horizon to try to see the outline of the French coast.

The sky was clearer than it had been the day before, but there was a strange haze over the water. It wasn't a sea mist, though – it was smoke. Something rumbled in the distance and we saw the tiny silhouette of a plane moving across the sky, but it was too far away for us to see if it was ours or the enemy's.

'It was that newspaper article about the Treachery

Act that really upset him,' I said.

Mags nodded – she had seen the article too.

'He thinks they are going to prosecute her,' I said. 'He thinks they'll find her guilty.'

Mags shook her head, furious. 'But what *proof* have they got?'

'They don't need proof, Mags.' And my voice sounded like it belonged to someone else. 'They've got her confession.'

'*Her confession?*'

My heart was beating in my throat as I passed my sister the piece of paper that I had tucked beneath my pillow.

'What's that? Another letter from Mutti?'

I shook my head. 'It's the same letter. This is the second page. I found it on Pa's desk last night, hidden underneath yesterday's newspaper.'

'He hid it from us?'

'Yes.' I recalled the shocked expression on Pa's face when I had walked into the kitchen, and the peculiar way in which Mutti's letter had ended: *P.S. Remember . . .*

Mags read the missing second page:

'*. . . that I have told the detective everything he needs to know. I am ready now to write everything down and sign it. I will write that I am guilty. This is really the best way. I love you all so much.*

'But she can't be a spy! Not our Mutti . . .'

'I know,' I said.

When Mags gave the piece of paper back to me, I saw that her hand was shaking, just like mine.

She must have noticed the same thing. She put her arm around me and squeezed me hard. She hadn't hugged me for months. Suddenly I couldn't hold back my tears any longer.

'I don't understand any of it, Mags,' I sobbed.

'No,' she said. 'But if she's making a confession to the police, she *must* have done something, mustn't she?'

Pinstripe's ominous words echoed through me: *Sometimes, good people do bad things . . . This is something you are going to need to come to terms with. Very soon.*

Perhaps he had received her written confession already. I pulled away from my sister, wiped my eyes with my sleeve and sat still for a moment.

'What do you think will happen?'

'I don't know.'

It wasn't likely that the police would be looking for another suspect now – my sister, or Spooky Joe, or anyone else for that matter. They had a written confession from my Mutti – what more did they need? I didn't say anything about Joe's coded note or the fact that Mags's initials had been on it; as far as Mags was concerned, the scrap of paper had been lost somewhere between the south cliff and Dragon Bay.

She took a breath. 'We just have to wait to see what the police will do. Mutti will probably be transferred from the camp to a prison, and then there will be a trial . . .' She stopped. She didn't want to think about what happened after that. **TRAITORS TO BE HANGED** . . . The sea below us was swilling back and forth against the cliff – I was a ship in a bottle being tipped this way and that.

'There's nothing we can do right now, Petra.' Mags paused. 'Nothing we can do for Mutti, anyway . . .' And I saw that she was looking towards France again. She was thinking about all those poor soldiers caught between the devil and the deep blue sea.

'You want to go and help them.'

'Yes,' she said. 'I do. Now more than ever.'

Mags got to her feet and held out her hand to pull me up beside her. We stood there together, quite still, hand in hand, looking out to sea, and I became aware of a strange, high-pitched resonance, a fierce energy filling the air all around us. Just for a moment, there weren't four Daughters of Stone on our clifftop: there were six of us.

When we went back into the kitchen Pa was still sitting in his chair. He was bent double now, with his head in his hands. He didn't even look up when we came in. 'I can't take it, Mags,' he said. 'Don't ask me again. I just can't . . .'

Mags looked at him. For a moment, I was afraid that she was going to swear or storm out again, but she didn't. She knelt down on the floor next to Pa. When she spoke, her voice was soft. 'I want to help, Pa – we can't just let this happen, can we? I can't join up to fight, but I know how to man a boat. This is something I can actually do to make a difference. Please, Pa.' She put her hand on Pa's arm. 'We can't help Mutti right now, but we can do this – we can help *them*.' Pa was still looking at the floor, his hands pressed over his eyes. When he looked back at my sister, I saw that his face was wet with tears. I had never seen my father cry before. A vast pit of fear opened up inside me.

'I'll go, then,' he said, his voice hoarse. 'I'll go. And you can help me, Magda. Is the motor boat in working order yet?'

Mags shook her head. 'Not really, Pa.' I could tell she was disappointed that she wouldn't be going too, but she didn't want to upset Pa again.

'Then get down to the harbour and give the old lifeboat the once-over for me.' His voice shook and he swallowed hard. 'I'll set off with the tide first thing tomorrow.'

'Tomorrow?'

'Yes,' Pa said. He sounded determined now. 'Tomorrow. There's something very important I need to do first.'

24

With Mags down at the harbour working on the old lifeboat, and Pa up in the service room, I was left in charge of dinner. Since Mutti had gone, we had taken it in turns to cook, and I wanted to make the three of us a special meal that night as a surprise for Pa. The trouble was, the more I tried to make it special, the more it felt like a last supper. I kept blinking back tears that welled up out of nowhere.

I was peeling potatoes at the sink when I saw a movement out of the corner of my eye – someone was in our garden – and then, before I could catch my breath, there was a sharp rapping sound on the door. I jumped, and the potato knife slipped in my wet hand, slicing through the soft pink skin under my thumbnail.

I cursed under my breath and dried my hands as best I could, wrapping a clean cloth around my bleeding thumb. By the time I opened the door, my heart was flipping about like an eel.

It was Pinstripe.

'Oh. Hello,' I said.

'Hello.'

And then Pa's voice was in the kitchen behind me. 'I wasn't expecting you to come up here to find me, Inspector,' he said. His voice was oddly formal – the same tone he used when he spoke to the Admiralty on the telephone, but more stilted.

'Well, I thought I'd save you the trouble of coming down to the station,' the detective said, removing his hat. 'And there was always the risk that you might . . . change your mind.'

Change his mind about what?

Pinstripe gave me one of those looks that grown-ups are very good at, and said, 'Perhaps you could leave us to have a little chat in peace, Petra?'

I looked at Pa. *What's going on? Is it something to do with Mutti?* But his face wore a strange, hard expression – all closed up. His hands gripped the top of the kitchen chair too tightly.

I went away, leaving them to their 'little chat'. I didn't go to my room, though. I had a plan. I unbolted the heavy door that linked the cottage to the light-house, feeling the chill of the concrete through my socks. I crept up the stairs.

Up in the lantern room, I went straight to the speaking tube, carefully removed the brass whistle and put the funnelled end to my ear. I sat down, trying not to breathe too loudly. I stared out through the glass into the blue of the day, and listened.

'I had been waiting to hear from you, Mr Smith.' That was Pinstripe. He must have been sitting a bit further away from the speaking tube – on the other side of the table; his voice was quieter than Pa's.

'Waiting? Then you knew?'

I caught my breath. *Knew what?*

'I've had suspicions since I came here to the light-house on the day of your wife's tribunal. We took one of your old logbooks, and I've been comparing your charts with the diagrams we seized.'

'Ah.'

A cold, sick feeling started spreading through my body.

'I needed stronger proof and was about to bring you in for questioning when I received your telephone call.'

Proof? Was he saying it was Pa? That *Pa* was the traitor? But . . .

'I only sent that one package, sir. Just one package of information.'

My heart pounded so hard I thought it might burst.

I saw that the blood from the cut under my thumbnail was soaking, bright red, through the cloth.

'But why, Mr Smith? You're not on the side of the Nazis, are you?'

Of course he's not, I wanted to scream down the tube. *Of course he's not!* I pressed my clammy hand over my mouth to stop myself from screaming it out loud.

But Pa didn't say anything.

'Why now? Why tell me the truth now?'

Pa cleared his throat. 'You know why. My wife has made a confession. And with the new Treachery Act – the sentence . . . It's all lies, of course – her confession. She must be trying to protect me. She must have found out somehow.'

'Yes, perhaps,' Pinstripe said. 'She is certainly trying to protect someone. I went to see her yesterday and told her we wouldn't be using her confession as evidence, as it clearly wasn't true. She was not able to replicate the diagrams or even explain the meaning of the shipping coordinates.'

The world beyond the window was a swimming haze of sea and sky. I felt as if I were clinging to the top of a mast, swaying sickeningly above the real world. It was all too much – Mutti's confession, and now Pa's. It seemed now that Mutti's life was saved, but Pa – *my Pa* . . .

'Why did you do it, Mr Smith? Who contacted you?'

Pa said nothing for a few moments. Then he just said, 'I had no choice. That is all I am able to say, Inspector. I had no choice.'

'What do you mean exactly?'

'I mean that if you were torn between loyalty to your country and love for your family, what would you choose? What would you *actually* choose?'

Pinstripe said quietly, 'I'm afraid I couldn't say, Mr Smith. But in the eyes of the law, you have committed treason. You know that, don't you?'

'Yes,' Pa said. 'I understand.'

The pulse in my jaw throbbed against my fingers. A drop of blood fell from my thumb and splashed on to the concrete floor of the lantern room.

Pinstripe had known it was my Pa. When he said that good people do bad things, he hadn't been talking about Mutti at all . . .

'There's just one thing I need to ask,' Pa said. 'I realize this is probably not something you are allowed to do, Inspector, but I need to ask you not to arrest me today. Could you give me, please, until tomorrow night?'

I heard Pinstripe's chair shifting on the floor. He tried to interrupt, but Pa kept talking.

'I'm not going to do anything else, sir – you have my word. I sent one package and that is all I ever intended to send. There are no more secrets I can share. There is no more damage I can do. But I can do something else

– something good.'

'What are you proposing?'

'Let me take the lifeboat over to Dunkirk to help rescue our boys,' Pa said. 'They've been appealing on the wireless – anyone able to handle a boat. Well, that's me. I can do something good. Please, Inspector. I'm not asking you as a policeman, I'm asking you as a man. My daughter Magda is so desperate to go, but I can't let her – and I know that if I don't go, she will. She's full of fire, but she's so young. Let me go. Let my last act in this war be one that *saves* lives. *Please* . . .'

There was a terrible strain in Pa's voice now, a wheezing and cracking, and I realized that he was crying again. There were tears running down my cheeks and both my hands were shaking, but I still kept the speaking tube clamped tightly to my ear, even though my right arm was now numb and bloodless. I tried not to sniff. I couldn't let them hear me.

'And what happens when you get back?' Pinstripe said after a moment.

'When I get back, I'll walk straight into the police station and turn myself in.'

Everything was quiet for a moment. I tried to imagine what was happening. Perhaps the two of them were shaking hands. There was the sound of chairs moving on the kitchen floor, and then I heard the door open and close, and there was silence again.

I replaced the brass whistle in the end of the

speaking tube, and hung it from its bracket on the wall. The blood surged back into my deadened arm like molten lead.

25

Pa woke me before dawn the next morning. He didn't mean to, but I heard the floorboard sigh as he came past our room. Mags was still fast asleep.

'It's all right,' he whispered. 'Don't get up, Pet. I'm just going out in the boat for the day. I'll be back tonight.'

Had he forgotten that I was there when he said he would take the lifeboat to Dunkirk? Perhaps he wanted to convince me that what he was doing was not dangerous at all – just a spot of fishing on an early summer's day. Or perhaps he was trying to convince *himself*.

'Take care, please, Pet,' Pa said. 'Look after the lighthouse, and look after that stubborn sister of yours too. Remember to go straight into the cellar if you hear the air-raid siren or planes overhead.'

'Yes, Pa,' I said.

'Promise me.'

'I promise.'

I wanted to reach out to him with both arms like I did when I was tiny. I wanted him to scoop me up so I could tuck my knees against his chest and bury my face in his shoulder. I couldn't bear the thought of him going so far away, sailing straight into the clutches of Hitler's army. And I couldn't bear the thought of him coming home, only to turn himself in at the police station as a traitor. I had hardly slept a wink that night. *Pa*, the voice in my head whispered. *Pa is the traitor* . . . And then that dreadful headline again – **TRAITORS TO BE HANGED** . . .

'I'll see you tonight, then, my darling,' he said, bending over to kiss me on the forehead.

The floorboard creaked as he turned away, and after a few seconds I heard the kitchen door open and close.

I shut my eyes and tried to get back to sleep.

I don't know how long I lay there, my tired eyelids flickering in the gloom, but eventually I gave up on sleep altogether, threw back the blanket and went over to my sister's bed.

'Mags,' I whispered. I don't know what I was going to say to her, I just knew I couldn't bear to be alone in the darkness any more. Should I tell her about Pa, about what I had heard through the speaking tube? I sat down on the edge of her bed and touched the shoulder-shaped lump of blanket. 'Mags . . . ?'

But there was no shoulder beneath my hand, there was only blanket and pillow.

Mags wasn't there.

It was a hideous moment, like biting into an apple that turns out to be soft and rotten inside. I pulled the blanket right back, just to be sure, and there on her bedsheet was a note addressed to me:

Pet,

I'm going to Dunkirk. Pa doesn't know, so please don't tell him — I'm hoping to get back before he does, so he won't even have a chance to be worried or angry. I have to go too, Pet. Do you remember when I left school, and I said that history was happening all around us? This is my chance to be part of it. I know that I am meant to do this, and I know you will understand.

I'm taking the motor boat — I did some work on the engine yesterday afternoon and got it running nicely. She'll be just fine. I know she'll look after me, Pet, so try not to worry too much.

We'll both be home tonight.

Love from Mags x

No, no, no, Mags . . . The note shivered between my finger and thumb, and I noticed that my knife-cut from the day before had healed into a thick black scab under my nail. My breathing was shallow and panicky. *Light* — I needed light, and air. I pulled up the blackout blind, flung open the window, and was dazzled by the brightness of the day outside.

Inside me, though, everything was still dark and cold and terrifying.

I was completely alone.

I couldn't bring myself to eat any breakfast. Instead, I went up to the lantern room with a blanket around my shoulders, opened up Pa's brass telescope, and put it to my eye.

I watched all the boats leaving Stonegate harbour — a little flock of them — fishing boats, mainly, but some sailing boats too and a couple of private motor boats. They were joined further out to sea by bigger vessels from Dover, Folkestone, Deal and Ramsgate — leisure boats, yachts, paddle steamers . . . *All these people*, I thought. *All these people, setting off across the Channel to help rescue our soldiers.*

I filled in Pa's logbook, trying to find a bit of comfort in this familiar responsibility. I recorded the date, the weather, and the details of as many of the Dunkirk boats as I could. I knew plenty of them by name.

I saw the old lifeboat, and the dark, squarish figure of my Pa steering her out of the harbour. The urge to call to him swelled in my throat – he looked so close through the telescope! – but I knew there was no way that he would be able to hear me. Some way behind him – *a safe distance behind*, I thought – I saw the rusty motor boat, *Faith*. Two strong feelings were fighting against each other: pride in my crazy, courageous sister, and anger at her for having deserted me. I allowed myself to feel both, watching the whole shoal of boats until their various shapes and colours began to be lost amongst the shifting patterns of sunlight on the waves. The smaller they became, the more I was aware of a painful, pulling sensation in my chest, as if someone had tied a rope around my heart and was tugging at it harder and harder.

I couldn't bear to watch any more. I was just about to head back down to the kitchen when one more boat caught my eye. It was one of the Briggs's family fishing boats, and it was zipping along at a terrific rate, chasing the wake of the last craft of the flotilla – my sister's rusty motor boat.

'Kipper?' I said out loud, taking up the telescope again. It *must* be. I had never thought of Kipper Briggs as the heroic type, but perhaps, just like Mags, he had decided that this was his chance to be part of history. He wanted to make a difference too.

Kipper's was the last boat to leave Stonegate. I

folded up the telescope and made my way down the lighthouse stairs, trying to think of ways to make the time between morning and evening pass quickly; I knew it was going to be hours and hours until they came back.

26

I fed Barnaby. I polished the lamp. I cleaned the cottage from top to bottom. I weeded the vegetable patch. I washed clothes and mangled them and hung them out to dry. I mended my torn coat. I did every little job I could find that needed doing, and it was still only four o'clock. The cottage was horribly quiet.

I locked up the main door to the lighthouse. We never really bothered locking the cottage door, but keeping the lighthouse secure was one of Pa's strictest rules.

I found my pencils and sketchbook in my room, and went to sit out on the clifftop. I had hardly drawn anything since Mutti had been taken away, but my head and my heart were so full this afternoon that it was the only thing I could think of that might make me feel a bit better.

I settled down on the dry grass with my back against the smallest standing stone. I drew the cliffs, the clouds, the water – flat, barren and grey – and the dull shape of the Wyrm, sleeping just below the surface. I drew myself as a tiny, hunched figure looking out across the sea towards the empty horizon. *I'll draw the Daughters of Stone*, I thought. But, when I did, something very odd happened. My hand didn't draw four ancient standing stones – it drew four girls, dressed in long white gowns. They were upright, defiant, their hair blowing in the wind, and their arms stretched out towards the sea. They stood, two of them either side of the tiny, hunched figure of Pet Smith. I rubbed out that pitiful little shape, and drew myself again, standing up with the Daughters, my hair blowing in the wind just like theirs. A high note trembled in the air like a thread of silver.

My skin prickled.

I drew a boat on the water, and another and another and, when I next looked up at the sea, I saw that something magical had happened. I dropped my sketchbook and pencils on the grass. *A miracle.*

The first one was white. Just the spray of a wave, perhaps, or a spark of reflected evening sun, but then it became clearer: an angular little shape, like folded paper, carving its way through the navy sea. A sailing boat. And after the first one, the other boats started appearing on the horizon – three, five, eight, twenty, fifty or more – just like my drawing . . . *There should be singing*, I thought, *a chorus. There should be a fanfare of trumpets. They are coming home – just look at them!*

Fishing boats, steamers, yachts, trawlers started to emerge from the haze. The decks of the larger ships and steamers were dark with army uniforms – hundreds of men crowded together. As the boats approached the coast, they fanned out – each heading to its own home harbour. I imagined the view from the perspective of one of the soldiers: the white cliffs of England opening up before them like a mother's arms. I waved to one of the boats, but I couldn't see if anyone waved back. I must have been a tiny little shape to them. The sun was setting behind me now. They would only be able to make out a dot on the clifftop. A dot, a tower and four old boulders.

Then I recognized one of the larger boats: the *Margate Queen*. She was a paddle steamer we had been on once during a summer excursion to Margate. It was so odd to see her in this way. The *Margate Queen* meant fish and chips, Punch and Judy, buckets and spades . . . And yet here she was – a warship: an enormous lifeboat, saving the lives of hundreds of men.

As the sun faded, it became colder up there on the clifftop. I fetched my blanket from the cottage and wrapped it around my shoulders and over my head to make a sort of tent.

What do I do if they don't come back tonight? my mind whispered anxiously. *What do I do if they never come back? Will I wait here for ever?*

What was the alternative? I couldn't face the idea of going back to sit in the empty kitchen by myself. It was better to wait here on the cliffs with the stones. I felt closer to Pa and Mags somehow.

Another cluster of boats. Then a long gap and a boat on its own, but it wasn't *Faith* or the lifeboat either; it was a little dinghy.

I gazed at it as the world darkened around me. Its sail was ragged with bullet holes and it felt like a terrible omen. There were no more boats on the horizon.

I pulled the blanket tightly around me and lay down on the cold grass. *I should try to get a little sleep*, I thought. But then I looked up at the thousands of stars in the vast sky above and shuddered. I closed my eyes tightly. *I don't think I can.*

But I must have, because when I opened my eyes again, I was stiff with cold, and the light had changed from black to a cool milky grey. A few pale stars still freckled the sky, but it was almost morning.

Had there been a shooting star? I couldn't remember if I'd seen it as I was falling asleep or if I'd dreamt it. I felt hollow and lost, haunted by the hours of dark, silent loneliness since Pa and Mags had left. I pressed my hands together, trying to squeeze some warmth into my freezing fingers. A strange, low mist crept across the sea.

They aren't coming home. They would be back by now if they were coming.

Then, without any warning, the idea was there in my head and I knew exactly what I had to do. I had to sing. Fear shivered through me as I turned towards the Daughters of Stone.

The fishermen's daughters sang a song of love and loyalty and sacrifice to bring their fathers safely home. This was the moment that I had always known about in my bones, ever since Pa first told me the legend. This was the moment in which I would finally become part of this ancient story. The sky wrapped around me, grey as fate, enveloping me, together with the stones and the cold-smoking sea.

I stood up, and started to sing. It was the German lullaby Mutti used to sing to me when I was a baby. My lips were dry and my voice shook – I had barely spoken out loud for a day and a night. I sang about the moon and the stars, shadows and mist – 'the world in stillness clouded, and soft in twilight shrouded'. I sang about being 'in His keeping' – protected and safe through the darkness . . .

I was aware of the stones all around me as I sang. I knew from the quickened pulsing of my heart that the ancient magic was not dusty and sleeping: it was alive, it was awake. I didn't need to look at the stones to know they were listening to me, their granite glittering like frost in the dawn light. Their song floated in the air with mine, a song like gauze or thistledown – I couldn't hear it; I *felt* it: fine and strange. The back of my neck prickled and my skin turned to goosebumps. My hair streamed in the wind, just as it had in my drawing. The sea breezes flapped around me like the beating of feathered wings, whipping the words from my mouth and carrying them away – out over the sea. Was the magic working?

Then I saw it. A boat, emerging from the mist, heading for our harbour.

I could hardly breathe. I just watched the boat coming closer and closer to the shore. *If it is the lifeboat*, I thought, *or the motor boat – if it is Pa or Mags – what will happen to me now? Will the Wyrm take my soul? Will I turn to stone?* I wrapped my arms around myself. My skin felt numb – rough and goosebumpy. Perhaps it was happening already.

Fingers of mist reached up towards me from the sea . . .

It is the lifeboat! And, for a moment, I really believed that it was.

Your brain can do terrible things to you when you are in that sort of state – when you are desperate for something to be true. To this day, I could swear that I saw the dark blue and white paintwork, the red trim, the little flag at the front . . .

But I saw no such thing. It was not the lifeboat at all. It was Kipper's fishing boat.

Kipper was safely home, then, but not Mags, and not my Pa.

The sun kept rising slowly. At least it seemed to – I couldn't see the sun itself – it was hidden, like a burning face behind a widow's veil of smoke. The horizon glowed red and the sky reddened too. The scraps of cloud drifting above were as ragged as the sail of that little dinghy, shot through with bullets, crimson.

Two figures were walking slowly up the cliff path towards the Castle. A gull screamed in the blood-red sky. I squinted in the gloom. *Pa? Mags?* But I hadn't seen either of their boats return . . .

It wasn't Pa.

It was Kipper and, leaning heavily against him, was Mags.

She had a blanket wrapped around her, her jumper was ripped and she had a cut on her arm. She walked as if her legs could barely take her weight. Kipper helped her up the steep slope to the Castle. I ran to my sister and clung to her tightly. Her clothes were cold and wet. Her face, beneath blackened smudges, was bloodless.

She looked as if she needed to say something, but she couldn't say it. She just stared at me.

I stared back, a huge sob rising painfully in my chest as I realized what this meant. I put my arms around my sister again, pressing my face into her shoulder as I said the words she couldn't say.

'Pa isn't coming home, is he.'

27

Mags had a bath and then fell deeply asleep, curled up on her bed in her striped pyjamas.

Kipper helped me make tea in the kitchen. We ate corned beef sandwiches made with the last of the week's stale loaf.

'Tell me what happened, Kipper.'

'Where do you want me to start?' he said.

'At the beginning.'

'Right. Well – I wasn't planning on going to Dunkirk. Mum's found things very difficult since Dad was . . . you know . . .'

I nodded. I understood why he didn't want to say it out loud.

'Well, I said I wouldn't go. I was down at the

harbour early morning yesterday, helping our lads get the boats ready for the trip, when I saw Mags there, fiddling with her clapped-out old motor boat. It never occurred to me that she was actually planning on crossing the Channel in that rust-bucket. Anyway — pretty much everyone else had left, and I was just about to head home to Mum when I heard Mags start up the motor and I saw her and the rust-bucket go chugging out of the harbour.'

'What did you do?' I knew the answer to that question already.

'There was one of our boats still moored up. I jumped straight in and followed her,' he said. He couldn't look at me then, just kept his eyes fixed on the flagstone floor. 'I know boats, and I knew that boat would never make it to France.'

'She *did* make it to France,' said a voice at the doorway. 'She just didn't make it home again.'

Mags was awake.

'Come and sit by the stove, Mags,' I said. 'You need to keep warm.'

She sat down beside me, and we huddled close together like spooked sheep. I inspected the wound on her arm and changed the dressing, wrapping a clean bandage around and around, and fixing it with a safety pin.

'So *Faith* did make it to Dunkirk,' I prompted.

'Only just,' murmured Kipper.

'The crossing was fine,' Mags said quietly. 'There were lots of planes in the sky, though. I saw a German fighter brought down by Hurricanes, and another by the guns on a minesweeper.'

'That was where I lost you – in the confusion of that plane coming down,' said Kipper. 'We still had a couple of miles to go till the French coast when I last saw you in the rust-bucket.'

Mags gave him a look.

'In *Faith*, I mean.'

'She packed up about a mile from Dunkirk, just after I passed the minesweeper,' Mags said. 'The engine puttered out and stopped, and there was nothing I could do to get her started again.'

'What did you do?'

'A very kind man helped me.'

'Who?'

'Our Pa.'

'*Pa* found you?'

'He had spotted me behind him and was already on his way back to meet me when I broke down. I imagine he was planning on sending me straight home, but when it became clear the motor boat wasn't going anywhere, I joined him in the lifeboat and we towed *Faith* behind us. I think he was very angry with me, but he didn't say anything. He seemed sort of . . . *proud* as well as angry.'

I knew exactly how he felt.

'When we got to France, the soldiers were lined up on the beaches, waiting to be collected. It reminded me of playtime at school, when we were little. The teacher rang the bell and we would line up on the field to go back into the classroom. Do you remember?'

'Yes.'

Kipper nodded too. School felt like something from another lifetime. We were different creatures now.

'There were dead bodies,' Kipper said in a low voice. 'Shot, or killed in explosions, or drowned and washed up on the sand. Some men looked like they'd given up hope and were sitting by themselves, all bent over and shaking. Others were trying to wade or swim out to the ships waiting in the deep water.'

'We could go right into the shallows to collect them, though,' Mags went on, 'because the lifeboat was so much smaller. We took fifteen men at a time – ten in the lifeboat itself and five in the motor boat, tagging along behind. We ferried them to the destroyers and paddle steamers. We must have taken a hundred men out to the *Margate Queen* alone.'

'I saw her,' I said. 'I saw the *Margate Queen* coming home.'

'They got back safely, then?'

'Yes.' Mags held her mug of tea against her chest, as if her heart needed the heat.

'One man was panicking in the water. A body floated past him – it had been burnt, I think – and this man just couldn't bear it. He started screaming and trying to swim out towards us. He dragged a man under and they both nearly drowned.'

'What happened?'

'Another soldier grabbed him and put a gun to his head. By the time he got on to the lifeboat he had gone completely quiet. He just sat there – rigid, like a statue. Even when a Spitfire flew low overhead, he didn't look up. When we got to the *Margate Queen*, he shook Pa's hand, but he couldn't say anything.'

'What did Pa say?'

Mags's voice faded to a hoarse whisper. 'He said, "Thank you, sir. And good luck." After the man had gone, Pa said to me, "We all have moments we live to regret. We have no idea what fear will do to us until it takes hold."'

Mags was quiet for a moment. Her breathing was all jumpy. Some of her tea slopped over her fingers and Kipper gently took the cup from her.

'Mags,' I said very softly. 'What happened to Pa?'

She stared at the floor. Her dark hair fell forward over her face.

'We were on our way home. We'd done our last run out to a destroyer and Pa said we should head back. To be honest, I think he was worried about you being here all by yourself.'

I almost laughed. *Pa was there, surrounded by bombs and dogfights and machine guns and dead bodies, and he was worried about me.*

'Then we hit a mine. The bow of the lifeboat exploded and we were both thrown into the water. It's just a terrible blur now — I-I don't really know what happened. I remember being underwater and not knowing which way was up. I took a lungful of water and I just thought, *This is the end, then.*'

'But it wasn't.'

'No. Something hit my arm and I lunged at it. I clung on. It was a boathook. I was hauled along and then a hand grabbed mine and pulled me up out of the water. It was Kipper.'

I looked at Kipper, and thought how odd it was to have him here with us in our kitchen. How different he seemed now from the boy I thought I knew.

'I heard the explosion,' Kipper said. 'Saw it too. I pulled Mags out and we looked for your dad.'

Mags looked at me and I saw a sob rise in her throat. One hand moved up to cover her mouth, as if she couldn't bear to let the words out. Then: 'We looked for ages, Pet. The lifeboat sank, and pulled *Faith* down with it. Bits of boat were bobbing around in the waves. After I'd got my breath, I went back into the water to see if Pa had been trapped or caught on something.' She swallowed, then she managed to say, 'He wasn't there. He wasn't anywhere. I couldn't find him.'

My throat was aching unbearably, and my chest too. I thought about the lullaby that I had sung to the sea as

I prayed for Mags and Pa. I had felt so sure that some kind of magic was working . . . *Just enough to bring Mags safely home*, I thought. *But not enough for my Pa.*

We sat in silence. Tears ran, one after another, down my face.

Kipper stood up and said quietly, 'I'll leave you two alone, I think. I'd better get back to my mum. I sent word with one of the lads that I was all right, but I'd better get back . . .' He trailed off. 'I'm really so sorry about your dad,' he said, and he went to the door.

'Thank you, Kipper,' said Mags.

He turned and nodded to her – holding her gaze for a moment – and then he left.

After a few seconds, I managed to smile and say, 'Kipper Briggs saved your life.'

Mags shook her head and I saw that she could not understand any of the things that had happened. She just said, 'He's a good sailor, Kipper. He can turn that boat on a sixpence. He'll make a fine captain one day.'

'Kipper the Skipper,' I said.

My sister attempted one of her grins.

'Were you looking for Pa all night, Mags?'

She shook her head. 'By the time we gave up the search, it was getting late. We couldn't come back the way we'd come – straight across the Channel – because we wouldn't have been able to avoid the mines in the dark – or the sandbank, for that matter – so we had to take a different route, a much longer one. We went north-east before crossing the Channel somewhere near Essex and then coming back down the English coast in the early hours of this morning. That route probably saved our lives.'

The magic of the stones helped too, I thought. But I didn't say it out loud.

Then, quite suddenly, Mags gasped and said, 'I'm so sorry, Pet – I'm sorry I couldn't save our Pa. He wouldn't even have been there if I hadn't . . .'

I put my arms around my big sister's middle, like I used to when I was a little girl.

I hugged her, but I couldn't say anything at all, because these are the words that were in my head: *Pa drowned in the sea between England and France. He is never coming home. But now he will never be tried as a traitor and no one will ever need to know what he did. I won't tell Mags, and I won't tell Mutti. I will keep his terrible secret all by myself and I will never let it go – it is my secret to keep for the rest of my life. And, no matter how much it burns, I will hold on to it tightly.*

PART THREE

Summer 1940

28

'There's no question, I'm afraid,' Mrs Baron went on. 'I'm terribly sorry about your father, of course, girls, but I have a duty to ensure you are both safe and looked after, and you simply cannot stay here alone.'

She sat down, tucking her legs beneath the kitchen table. She was wearing a grey-brown cardigan. I was reminded of a kestrel again – the neatness of her, the precision of her bright, darting gaze. She seemed genuinely concerned, but that didn't make it any easier to accept what she was saying. She turned now towards the lady she had brought with her – Mrs Peacock, from the local authority.

'Don't worry! We will be able to accommodate you both somewhere,' Mrs Peacock said chirpily, picking up her cue. 'There is always a way!' She examined a piece of paper she had placed on the table, but had to lean forward slightly to read it as it was eclipsed by her enormous bosom. She tutted. 'Given the circumstances, fostering doesn't seem to make sense — we might as well just sign them up for the evacuation programme. If you'd gone a bit earlier, we might have been able to squeeze you both in together somewhere, but with things as they are now, it will probably have to be separate arrangements . . . Mags—'

'Magda,' my sister corrected sharply.

'Magda,' Mrs Peacock repeated, smiling at Mags very deliberately. 'You're a strong, useful girl and you're pretty tall too. I think there might be a place for you working on a farm. You're a bit young to be a Land Girl as such, but we could probably make it work . . . Now, Pet—'

'Petra.' My sister again.

'Yes.' Mrs Peacock cleared her throat. 'At the moment, it is looking likely to be Shropshire.'

'Shropshire?' I blurted out. 'Where is that, please? Is it by the sea?' A sudden panic took hold of me. I was imagining being trapped *inland*, away from the sea and the clifftops and the never-ending sky. I would never have said this out loud, but I felt that my Pa was part of the sea now. I felt that leaving the Castle would be a terrible betrayal: I would be abandoning the lighthouse and abandoning Pa too — leaving him behind.

'Of course Shropshire's not by the sea,' Mrs Peacock scoffed. 'Don't you know the geography of your own country, young lady? It's between England and Wales. A beautiful county.'

I looked down at my shoes.

Mrs Peacock studied her piece of paper again. 'In fact, there's a very nice elderly couple in Shropshire who would apparently be happy to consider a longer-term arrangement. They have asked for an orphan—'

'We're not orphans,' said Mags, quick as an arrow.

There was a horrible pause. I felt my chest rising and falling quickly. I wanted to hide, but I just kept looking at my shoes.

'No, dear,' Mrs Baron said soothingly.

'Our mother is not dead.'

'Of course she isn't.' The eyes of the two women met fleetingly.

There was a feeling inside me that threatened to bubble up into words, but I swallowed it back down. It was a dangerous, treacherous feeling. *I feel like an orphan*, I wanted to say. *I feel like there is no one here to protect me.* For some reason, I thought about that day when I was scurrying across the cliffs with Mrs Rossi's umbrella, convinced I was about to be struck by lightning. I felt just like that now – exposed, vulnerable. Anything could happen.

When Mrs Peacock spoke again, her tone was different – firmer, as if to put an end to Mags's nonsense. 'The evacuation programme has been a tremendous success thus far.' She folded her arms across her bosom and tucked in her chins. 'Many thousands of children have been happily and safely rehomed already.' She whispered to Mrs Baron then, 'Did you know the government refer to it as *Operation Pied Piper* – I think that's charming, don't you?'

Mrs Baron smiled politely and then tried to reason with us: 'Now that we've had to withdraw our troops from France, the German invasion could happen any day, girls – any day!' Her eyes shone with an emotion I couldn't quite place. What was it? *Alarm?* 'The government are trying to get as many youngsters away from the south-east coast as possible. It's highly likely that this is where Hitler's army will land—'

'Operation Pied Piper?' Mags interrupted. She was still staring at Mrs Peacock. '*That's* what they're calling the evacuation programme?'

I flinched, recognizing what Mutti called Mags's 'challenging' voice.

'And what of it?' Mrs Peacock replied, her smile rather brittle now. 'All the little children dancing merrily out of the town? It's perfect!'

'But they never come back,' Mags said, glaring at her. 'That's the whole point of the story. In most versions of the legend *the children never come back*. In one version, the Piper drowns them all in the river. He steals the children as an act of revenge, because the

Mayor won't pay him after he gets rid of the rats. It's a story about greedy, untrustworthy bureaucrats. Whoever named the evacuation programme Pied Piper is *stupid*.'

Mrs Peacock started flapping about like a flustered pheasant. 'Well. I don't think there's any need for that sort of speculation, Magda, but I'm pleased to see that you've been paying attention in your English Literature lessons . . .'

'Our mother told us the story, actually. Robert Browning's poem is based on a *German* folk tale. Or didn't you know that either?'

'All right, Magda,' Mrs Baron said. 'That's enough.'

My sister was just lashing out now – angry that our lives were being taken out of our hands: we were being dragged away from our Castle and there was nothing we could do. Part of me was pleased to see Mags getting Mrs Peacock on the ropes, but I knew it wasn't going to change anything. First Mutti had been taken away from us, then Pa, and now we were going to be separated from each other and sent away. Things were beyond our control. Lightning was crackling in the sky above us and there was nowhere to hide.

Mags's face changed quite suddenly. It reminded me of the moment when Pa pushed up the lever and switched off the lighthouse lamp. 'Thank you so much for all your help and hard work, Mrs Baron and Mrs Peacock. But you're extremely busy ladies, I know –

I'm sure you will need to be getting along. I'll discuss the situation with my sister . . .' She escorted them both to the door.

Mrs Baron smiled a little, pulling on her gloves. 'You're good girls really,' she said. 'And you've had a terrible time of it. We'll find somewhere nice for you. And you mustn't worry about your lovely lighthouse. I shall get in touch with the coastguard and *personally* ensure that everything is well looked-after while you are away. I promise.'

Then Mrs Peacock opened the door and very nearly trod on Barnaby, who was sitting on the doorstep, waiting to come in. He leapt away from her with a yowl and flew down the garden like a ginger comet.

As soon as the door was closed again, Mags exploded: 'The nerve of that woman! We're not going *anywhere*, Pet.'

'But, Mags, you heard what Mrs Baron said – we're minors and we can't be left here on our own.'

'I don't care. I don't *care* what the bloody Baron said. We're staying right here where we belong, Pet.' Her dark eyes were aflame with anger. 'I'll find a way.'

29

Mags and I were sitting together up at the top of the lighthouse, nibbling sandwiches and talking quietly as it grew darker outside. The sunset had been astonishing – dark mauve, lavender, lilac . . . A red sky meant good weather the next day – I knew that, but I didn't know what a purple sky meant. There was something unearthly about the colour, something violent. It made me think of the black eye Mags had got at school the day the war began.

Pa's absence was all around us in the lantern room – an aching shadow. I kept expecting to hear the sound of his boots coming up the lighthouse steps, or his cheery, tuneless whistle. Neither of us could bear to talk about him. I knew it would be too much for Mags: I was sure that she felt Pa's death even more than I did: she felt it was all her fault. That morning, we had sent a letter to Mutti in her internment camp, telling her about everything that had happened – Dunkirk, Pa, and now the fact that we were going to be sent away from the Castle.

Mags and I had spent every minute trying to come up with a plan that might mean we could stay put, but nothing had convinced Mrs Baron so far. We were at the point of giving up.

'She's an interfering *old dragon*,' Mags spat.

'She's just trying to look after us and do her job, isn't she?' I replied, trying my best to keep a lid on my sister's temper. I was half-afraid that she'd storm down to Mrs Baron's house in the village and call her an *old dragon* to her face. Lord knows what would happen then – we'd probably be shipped off to Shropshire before our feet could touch the ground. 'Let's try talking to her again – or could one of the other grown-ups in the village help? There must be *someone* we know who can convince Mrs Baron to see things differently.'

Mags appeared to think about it for a moment, then she stood up and gathered our plates. 'I'll take these down to the kitchen,' she said. 'Then I might go out for a walk to clear my head.'

'But it's getting dark, Mags,' I called after her as she disappeared down the stairs. '*Mags?*'

She didn't reply. I heard the kitchen door slam shut.

I sat there on my own for a while, staring out over the dark sea, trying to think of something that might convince Mrs Baron to let us stay, but my brain felt blunt and tired, and all I could think about was Pa and Mutti.

Everything was very, very still and quiet, so I was confused when the wail of the Stonegate air-raid siren came drifting up over the cliffs. I scanned the bruised horizon with Pa's telescope.

Nothing.

It must be a false alarm.

I moved all around the lighthouse, checking each section of the coast with the telescope. The last rays of sunlight were disappearing in the west now, and the sky was a murky purple colour. There were no lights to be seen at all inland – it was after the blackout and, as far as most people were concerned, we were having an air raid . . .

But then there *was* a light – or at least I thought there was. Something seemed to flash on the farmland to the north-west of the lighthouse. Then it was gone again, and the gloom surged back like squid-ink. Had I imagined the light? I searched with the telescope again but could see nothing at all.

Then there was a sound. A low, familiar drone. I turned back towards the sea.

It was just a thin, dark shape at that point – barely visible in the heathery twilight. It could have been a gull or a goose, but it wasn't. I knew exactly what it was.

A bomber.

My breathing quickened. My fingertips started to tingle.

Just a second later, the heavens split apart and a fighter plane ripped through the sky above me, heading straight for the German bomber. I gasped at the noise – it was as if it were only inches above my head.

'Spitfire,' I murmured, transfixed.

I knew I should have gone straight down to the cellar, but I couldn't move.

The last of the light drained from the sky as the planes met over the bay. The Spitfire wheeled around the bomber like a mobbing magpie, and the sky rattled with guns. Three dark shapes dropped from the bomber, thumping heavily into Dragon Bay – two into the sea and one on to the beach itself – and then the plane started streaming smoke.

There was another plane now – from nowhere – a German fighter was bearing down on the Spitfire, its guns blazing. Even in the gloom of nightfall, I could see that the front part of the enemy plane was painted a startling bright yellow, like the beak of a bird of prey. The Spitfire dived sharply and headed out over the sea, drawing the German fighter away from our coast.

Smoke was still pouring from the injured bomber. It banked around and then, like a huge white rose opening, a parachute bloomed in the air. The bomber plunged steeply into the sea with a tremendous white crash of water.

A tiny figure hung beneath the parachute, helpless. I held my breath.

There was a very odd moment of calm. The moon was visible – large and low – and its pale light made the parachute into a ghost. The seconds were slower, the skies were silent, and the parachute floated down through the smoke, towards the silver sea.

What's that? I put the telescope to my eye again quickly.

In the shallows, just off the south beach, I saw the shape of a rowing boat, and two oars dipping and rising, dimpling the dark water.

Someone else must have seen the dogfight too. Someone else must have watched the bomber go down and the slow drift of the ghostly parachute. Whoever it was must be going out to rescue the Luftwaffe pilot.

I squinted hard through the telescope, and adjusted the focus.

Then I stopped breathing.

It was too dark to see the name *King Edward* on the prow of the little boat, but I didn't need to. I knew the shape of its hull, the pattern of its painted stripes.

But it wasn't the boat itself that had made my lungs tighten so painfully; it was the tall, square-shouldered silhouette that was rowing it out to sea.

Pa?

30

I don't know how I did it, but I did. My limbs prickled with pins-and-needles and my breathing was dangerously fast and gasping, but I managed to stagger down the lighthouse stairs and out of the cottage.

I knew that it couldn't possibly be Pa in the rowing boat – how could it be? – but I needed to *see*. If it wasn't Pa, then who was it? I could believe that the light flickering up on the north cliff had been some sort of illusion, but could I really have hallucinated a whole boat, and a person rowing it too?

I half-ran, half-fell all the way down the cliff path to the harbour. There were points at which I was aware of the ground thudding beneath my numb feet, and points at which I felt I was almost flying through the darkness. If Mrs Baron had seen me, racing along with a torch after the blackout, I would have been in serious trouble, but she wasn't anywhere to be seen.

I arrived at the beach, blood pounding, muscles burning. I stopped, hands on my knees and breathing hard, beside a huge crater in the sand. The bomb had missed the harbour, and it had missed the army buildings on the clifftop too, but it had blown a hole in the barbed wire over fifty yards wide. It looked as if a gigantic sea monster had taken a bite out of the beach.

Then I saw a long, thin groove in the sand. *This is where he launched from.* The groove ran all the way down to the water. There were footprints too – man-sized boots.

I looked out to sea, but there was no sign of the parachute, the pilot or Pa. There was hardly any breeze now. It was eerily still and the sea was calm. The moonlight sketched pencil-silver waves on the black silk of the surface. Then I heard the splash-and-creak of oars, quiet and regular. There was a light, faint and quivering – a lantern, perhaps – and the outline of a boat gradually became clear. It moved towards us, gliding smoothly with each pull through the water.

The figure rowing the boat was square-shouldered, just like Pa – and he rowed the boat exactly as Pa would have done, but something wasn't quite right. The man's hair was white as smoke in the moonlight. Was it a ghost? I shivered as the little boat drew nearer.

I thought of the Wyrm lurking below the surface. I imagined the rotting masts of all those ships reaching up towards the boat like the bony fingers of the dead.

My heart was beating so fast that it just felt like a dull, dizzy buzzing in my ribcage. The wet sand sucked at my feet.

I could hear voices coming from the sea wall over by the harbour, but I couldn't drag my eyes from the boat that was drawing closer and closer with each smooth pull of the oars.

Then it reached me, sliding up on to the sand with a gritty hiss.

The figure in the boat turned around and looked straight at me.

It wasn't Pa – of course it wasn't – but the floundering disappointment was shocked out of me almost immediately.

It was a face I recognized.

'*Spooky Joe*,' I breathed. Everything was so strange and so dreamlike, the words escaped from my lips before I could stop them.

The old man raised his bushy white eyebrows at me. 'Spooky Joe? That's what you call me, is it, Petra?'

I stared at him. How did he know my name?

My hands gripped the side of the *King Edward*. 'What are you doing in our boat?' I managed to say.

'*Your* boat, is it?' For a moment, I thought he was going to snarl at me, but then he stopped and shook his head, as if to say, *That's not important now.* He turned towards the dark shape that was slumped in the bottom of the boat.

I peered in.

'He's breathing, but he's unconscious,' Spooky Joe said.

A lantern had been placed in the bow of the boat. Its feeble light illuminated the face of a young man, who lay there, perfectly still. His hair and uniform were soaked through with seawater and there was something dark running down the side of his head and neck. Blood. *He can't be much more than twenty years old*, I thought. Just a few years older than Kipper Briggs or Michael Baron.

The voices were closer now. Two men in military uniform were half-running towards us from the direction of the harbour. The light from their torches whirled around on the sand like Catherine wheels.

'He'll be all right, I think,' said the first man after he had examined him. 'Taken a bash to the head, but he seems to have a strong enough pulse. Good job you got him out of the water so quickly – he'd have drowned otherwise.'

Spooky Joe grunted. He helped manoeuvre the Luftwaffe pilot out of the boat, but I noticed that he wasn't gentle with him. The pilot's left leg fell heavily on to the sand and twisted behind him. One of the men in uniform poured a few drops of something on to the young man's lips. It smelled like brandy.

'He'll be useful, won't he?' Spooky Joe said in a low, emotionless voice. 'You might be able to get some information out of him.'

The first officer shrugged. 'We can try.'

Then the pilot stirred. His eyelids flickered and he muttered something in German.

'We need a translator down here,' the first officer said to the second as he rolled the boy on to his side and handcuffed his wrists together. 'As quickly as you can.'

The second man was already on his feet when I said, 'I can speak German.'

Spooky Joe and the two military men looked straight at me. It was as if I had suddenly become visible. It was hard to read the expressions on their faces, though. I was useful, but could I be trusted?

'Can you? What did he say, then?'

'He said something about a sign – a signal.'

The pilot's eyelids flickered as he rolled on to his back, and he muttered the same words again.

'A signal?'

'Yes,' I said. 'A signal.'

I looked up towards the dark cliffs that lay beyond the lighthouse.

Perhaps I hadn't imagined it. Perhaps I had seen a light flashing up there after all.

31

I was back home and in bed by the time Mags finally crept back into the cottage. It must have been very late.

'Did you see the bomber come down?' I whispered. I don't know why I whispered – there was no one else in the cottage for us to disturb.

I had been lying there, sleepless in the dark, thoughts of the German pilot, Spooky Joe and the mysterious signal from the clifftops all swimming around in my head. Pa had been the spy that Pinstripe had been searching for – I knew that – but there must be someone else too: someone else had cut the telephone lines and burnt down the village hall, and someone was now flashing a light during the blackout signalling to the enemy . . .

'Yes,' Mags said. 'We saw it come down.'

'We? Where were you, Mags? Who were you with?'

But she didn't say anything.

'Mags?'

She changed into her pyjamas and climbed into bed. I heard the rustle of her sheet and blanket as she pulled them up over her shoulder and turned away from me.

What was wrong with her? After a few minutes of silence, I rolled in the opposite direction – towards the window – so that our backs were facing each other. Eventually I gave in to sleep, allowing the dark dreams to flood back into my exhausted brain.

The day after that, Mags was out of the house at dawn and didn't come home until after supper time, and the same thing happened the next day too. I spent both days up in the lantern room, polishing the lamp, and recording the weather conditions and shipping movements in Pa's logbook. I stared out to sea, hypnotized by the slow-twisting shape of the Wyrm beneath the waves, trying to work out what had happened to my sister. Something had shifted again – she was just as she'd been before Dunkirk, back in the early spring, when I'd felt I hardly knew her at all. I needed to talk to her about being evacuated – had she managed to speak to someone about it? Had she sorted it out somehow? We hadn't heard anything from Mrs Baron for a couple of days now.

Perhaps that cold, lonely silence between us would have gone on for ever, if it hadn't been for what happened to Mrs Rossi and her husband.

The police came for them and took them away.

They weren't spies – they hadn't done anything wrong at all – but their home country, Italy, had now joined the war – on Hitler's side, not ours. With everyone in the country so angry and frightened and expecting an invasion at any minute, Mr Churchill had ordered the police to 'Collar the lot!' – anyone who could potentially be a supporter of the enemy; anyone born in the wrong country. It didn't matter now if you were a Category B or C enemy alien – you were likely to be rounded up for the internment camps, and some people were being deported too.

Someone in the village had written a terrible word on the door of the Rossis' bakery and had thrown stones through their window. I was there, trying to help Edie tidy up a bit, when the police came. It wasn't Pinstripe, it was a grey-haired officer from Dover. He was very polite to Mr and Mrs Rossi, but he wasn't interested in investigating the vandalism of their shop. It wasn't the vandals he had come to arrest. He told the Rossis that they would be safer in an internment camp than in their own home. I saw the tears shining in Mrs Rossi's brown eyes as she and her husband were led away, and I thought of her kindness to Mutti on the day Spooky Joe had called her 'Jerry': *Difficult for all of us, my dear . . .*

As soon as I got home, I told Mags what had happened, and I told her what I wanted to do. To my surprise, she agreed to help.

We went straight back down to the village with a bucket of soapy water, a scrubbing brush, some wood, a hammer and a bag of nails. Edie and I scrubbed the graffiti off the front door of the bakery, and Mags boarded up the broken windows. A few people watched us from the other side of the street, others pretended not to notice. One man spat on the pavement as he passed. We ignored them all.

It was a hot day – one of those un-British summer days when the pavement is like the bottom of an oven and the heavy air throbs with heat. The back of my neck got redder and redder in the sunshine, and the soapy water ran down my arms. It must have been low tide, because the whole village smelt of warm, rotting seaweed. I scrubbed and scrubbed, and scratched at the door with my fingernails. I was determined not to leave a trace of the vulgar painted letters behind. I was thinking about kind Mrs Rossi, and I was thinking about my Mutti too. I remembered the look that passed between Mrs Peacock and Mrs Baron when Mags insisted that we weren't orphans – *They might as well be orphans* that look had said. If Pinstripe knew that Mutti had not committed any act of treachery, she was safe from being prosecuted, but how long would it be until she was released from the internment camp?

With this new policy to lock up every enemy alien in the country, Mutti might not be allowed home until the end of the war. And when would that be? *It could be years and years* . . . I hardly noticed the tears that ran down my cheeks as I scrubbed at the ugly paint. The sun burnt away at my back.

Mal Bright, one of the fishermen, stopped and offered to help us. His son, Sam, had been killed in the evacuation of Dunkirk. He had been hit by machine-gun fire trying to help a soldier out of the water.

'Thank you, Mr Bright,' Mags said, as Mal held the plank of wood steady across the window frame. My sister hammered it into place, knocking nails into the corners.

'I was wonderin',' Mal said. 'It's my boy's funeral on Friday. Sam's funeral.'

Mags stopped hammering. I stopped scrubbing at the paint.

'I was wonderin', because you won't be able to have a funeral as such, if you two would like it to be a memorial for your dad too?'

Mags looked at me properly for the first time in days. I was suddenly aware of my sunburnt neck, my hot, tear-stained face. I nodded.

'Yes,' Mags said. 'That's kind of you, Mr Bright. I think we would like that very much.'

32

Friday was cooler than the rest of the week had been – the white clouds looked as if they had been combed upwards by the stiff breeze. I put on my smartest dress and brushed down my old black coat.

Mrs Baron and Michael were waiting in the church porch when we arrived. I noticed that Michael's gaze followed my sister from the church gate, all the way through the churchyard. I looked at Mags, trying to see whatever it was that he seemed to see. She was wearing a coat of Mutti's. With its belted waist and buttoned collar, and her hair all up with pins, I suppose she did look a bit more grown-up than usual.

They greeted us and Mrs Baron gave us both a little hug and a pat on the back. *She's not such a bad old stick*, I thought, remembering how angry Mags had been with her in the wake of the 'Peacock and the Pied Piper' incident. *She isn't an old dragon at all. She just wants us to be safe.*

'I need to talk to you afterwards, please, girls,' she said, readjusting herself after our hugs and tucking a strand of hair back beneath her smart black hat. 'I've got a bit of good news for you.'

Good news? To do with being evacuated? Did we really have to talk about that *today*?

Mags looked away, stony-faced. I tried to smile politely at Mrs Baron as we turned to enter the church, but I suspect my face may have been grimacing.

It was cold and dim inside, as gloomy as a tomb. Daylight struggled through the stained-glass window behind the altar – wine-red and bottle-green. We shuffled into our pew near the front. I hadn't been to church for ages – not since before Mutti was taken away – and the familiar smells swirled around me like the rising tide: old hymn books, cold stone, dust and candle wax. The air was heavy with stillness and quiet prayer.

The church filled up quickly – the whole village was there, I think. Someone started playing the church organ, and I was relieved; the quiet, respectful muttering was starting to make me nervous. My best dress was not warm enough for the chill of the church, and I found that I was somehow shivering and sweating at the same time. My fingertips had gone all pale and waxy, as if I didn't have enough warm blood in my veins to reach them. I didn't want to look at poor Sam Bright's coffin. It was so close to me that I could almost have reached out and touched the newly hewn wood. I kept thinking that it could so easily have been my sister in there.

I made myself fold my hands in my lap and I looked up into the vault above us. I thought, as I had many times before, that it looked exactly like the upside-down hull of a ship. Perhaps Noah's ark had capsized and we were all the poor creatures drowning in the flood.

Then the vicar walked up the central aisle and stood in front of the altar. The organ stopped and we all stood up. There was a moment of silence. The vicar spread his hands and opened his mouth to welcome us, but he didn't say anything – he just stared at the back of the church, his mouth a perfect O. The entire congregation turned around to see what had taken the vicar by surprise.

A man had come through the church door. He walked up the aisle towards us, starched and upright in a patched old suit and boots that shone like black mirrors. It was Spooky Joe. What was *he* doing here?

He must have attempted to tame his wild white hair; it looked exactly like the combed clouds in the sky outside. He nodded stiffly to a couple of people as he walked in, his jaw set tight and serious. The muttering began again, but it was a different sort of muttering now.

He sat down on the other side of the aisle, just behind the Brights, and stared straight ahead. Then he nodded slightly to the vicar – just a downward shift of his mouth and a dipping of his hooded eyelids – and the service began.

We sang one of my favourite hymns and two others that I didn't know very well. The vicar spoke about those who had given their lives to help others, and those who risked their lives now as the war continued. He spoke about light and darkness, about fighting together and the importance of standing up to the evil in our world. He said some nice things about Pa's work as a lighthouse keeper, and he spoke about Sam Bright being the best batsman on the village cricket team. *Bright*, I thought. *Sam Bright, and my Pa and his lamp – both of them shining in the darkness.* Mal Bright and his wife Sarah stood together in the pew opposite ours, his arm around her shaking shoulders. Sam had been their only child.

'The two men we say goodbye to today were nothing less than heroes,' the vicar said. I saw that there were tears running down my sister's cheek and, instinctively, I linked my arm through hers. She didn't pull away from me.

Heroes? I thought, and I felt Pa's terrible secret

flutter in my chest like a trapped bird. *No, Pa was a traitor. But I will never tell. I will never tell anyone what I heard through the speaking tube that day.* My ribs ached under the strain of it. *You need to be strong, Pet. You just need to be brave and strong.*

Outside the church, Mrs Baron was waiting for us, hovering near the memorial for the Great War. Michael wasn't there – he must have gone home already.

'What's the good news?' Mags demanded, buttoning up her coat. We were still some way down the path from Mrs Baron, and I had the feeling that my sister was going to make a scene. 'Do we really have to talk about it right now, Mrs Baron?'

'We've found space for you with a nice family in Wales,' the headmistress replied, beaming at us both as we drew nearer. She seemed to be ignoring my sister's second question, and the tone of her voice too. 'Well, they've got room for Petra, and they think you, Magda, should be able to lodge at a nearby farm.'

'We'd be living in different places?' My sister had never been what you'd call protective, but I thought there was suddenly something fierce and maternal in her voice. On reflection, it was probably just fierce. This was Mags, after all.

'Nearby, we hope. We can't promise, but lodgings for you nearby do look possible.'

'I see. Well, given that we don't really want to go

anywhere at all, it sounds far from ideal, Mrs Baron.' Where had this grown-up voice suddenly come from? 'We'll talk about it when we get home,' she went on. 'And we need to discuss the supervision of the lighthouse with the coastguard too. I'll let you know our decision next week.' Mags started to steer me down the path towards the gate.

But the expression on Mrs Baron's face had changed. 'I'm afraid that won't do, Magda.' She stepped to the side so that she was standing in our way. I felt my sister's arm twitch as she fought the urge to give our headmistress a shove. 'It's not up to you to decide, you see,' she went on. 'I'm so sorry, but I have had to make the decision for you. Of course, I'd like to be able to take our time over this and pick somewhere perfect for you both, but we don't have the luxury of time. You're both minors and you are currently living in a very dangerous situation with no adult supervision – the lighthouse could well be a target, for German bombers or even saboteurs. We cannot risk something terrible happening to the two of you in your mother's absence. And as you have no other family . . .'

At that point Spooky Joe walked past us, his eyes fixed on the churchyard gate.

'Good morning to you, Mr . . .' Mrs Baron began, but he just waved dismissively, as though swatting away a housefly – and kept walking.

Mrs Baron blinked. She was used to being treated

with respect. Her face flushed hotly beneath her neat black hat. There was to be no reasoning with her now; with his one, cold gesture, it seemed that Spooky Joe had sealed our fate.

'The bus leaves just after five o'clock this afternoon. You'll have to catch the London train at Dover, and then change again in London on to the overnight train to Wales. I'll telephone ahead to make sure someone is there to meet you in the morning when you get to Wrexham. Right now, you need to go home and pack. I'll give you more details when I meet you at the bus stop. Five o'clock sharp, please.'

We walked home in silence.

The morning's flock of white clouds had been shouldered out of the sky by a herd that were fatter, darker, angrier. The wind whipped at the sea, and a cold salt-spray stung our eyes as we made our way back up the cliff path to the Castle.

'What are we going to do, Mags?' I said. 'Are we really going to pack our bags and go to Wales like Mrs Baron said?'

When my sister looked at me, there was a wild look in her eyes that made my stomach go all cold. 'Over my dead body,' she said.

33

This was the plan. We'd pack up our things, take food and blankets too, and we'd go to Dragon Bay Cave to hide out there. Mrs Baron and the other authorities would just assume we had run away in order to stay together.

It wasn't exactly a solution to our problem, and we hadn't considered what we would do when we ran out of supplies or clean clothes, but Mags said it would at least buy us some time in which we could – hopefully – come up with a better idea.

I was ready before Mags was.

'Don't forget to lock up the main door to the lighthouse, Pet,' Mags called to me from our room.

'I won't.'

I put down a bowl of food scraps for Barnaby, and

some fresh water too. I thought perhaps I could get a message to Edie and ask her to come and look after him while we were away. He was nowhere to be seen, though. *Out chasing rabbits, as usual.* It felt wrong that we were leaving without saying goodbye to him.

I waited outside the kitchen door with my bag at my feet, my heart feeling bulky and unfamiliar in my chest. It was just after half past four. Mrs Baron would be heading to the bus stop to meet us soon. What would she do when she realized we weren't coming? I knew the answer already. She would be *very* cross. She would come here to look for us straight away. I felt a spasm of fear in my stomach.

I turned to look through the window at the time on the kitchen clock. Twenty to five now. We didn't have long. 'Hurry up, Mags!' I called.

I cupped my hands around my eyes, peering through the window to see if there was any sign of her.

It was when I stepped back again that I saw something odd reflected in the glass. An unexpected shadow behind me. A dark flash of movement. I turned quickly, but there was no one there.

It couldn't be Mrs Baron. Not yet. She'd be waiting for us at the bus stop, surely?

'*Mags?*' I called, wondering if, for some reason, my sister had decided to use the door to the lighthouse instead of the kitchen door. I walked around the side of the cottage towards the cliff edge. Hundreds of feet below, the sea churned chaotically, hurling itself against the chalk walls that our Castle stood upon. The dark sky seemed to be drawing down lower and lower, like a great black theatre curtain.

More quietly this time: '*Mags?*'

There was a noise to my right and, as I snapped my head around, I thought I saw a figure disappearing behind the nearest standing stone.

Then a hand fell heavily on my shoulder and I screamed.

'Pet – *good grief* – it's only me!' My sister was behind me, all buttoned up and ready to go. 'What's wrong?'

'Nothing – I thought I saw someone. There – by the stones . . .'

But the only movement to be seen near the stones was the dancing and bending of the long, pale grasses that surrounded them.

'You and your imagination, Pet. There's no one there. Come on – we need to get down to the cave before Mrs Baron comes looking for us.'

I tried to convince myself that it was an adventure. As we squeezed our way through the tunnel with an assortment of bags, I tried to pretend that Mags and I were playing some kind of childish game. We were camping out for the night; we were being smugglers or pirates; we were running away to sea. When we got to the cave, I lit the oil lamp while Mags found the driest area and made us up two beds out of the blankets she had brought. Then she opened one of the bags from the kitchen and produced a pile of freshly made jam sandwiches wrapped in paper. I suddenly realized how hungry I was. We sat down together on Mags's bed and devoured the sandwiches.

I looked at my sister then – with a big blob of jam at the side of her mouth – and I saw a flash of the old Mags. I grinned, pointing at the jam, but my mouth was too full of bread and butter and strawberry jam to say anything coherent, and we both ended up laughing through our noses.

We could have been any two sisters laughing together in that moment, but beneath the silliness of the moment and the excitement of our escape was the numbing fear that we were completely alone now; we had no idea what was going to happen to us.

I don't know what made me think of it then, but I went to my bag of clothes and brought out the photograph of Mutti and Pa's wedding. I had taken it from the coal cellar that morning, just before the funeral, thinking I might keep it in my bedroom, and I had decided to pack it at the last minute. To be honest, I just couldn't bear to leave it behind.

'Look, Mags,' I said, unwrapping the soft, woolly sleeves of an old jumper from around the chipped frame. 'It's Pa and Mutti when they got married.' I held it out to her.

She looked at it, and her eyes filled with tears. 'Oh, just look at our Pa,' she said, touching the glass. I looked at the young man with his gentle face and sticking-out ears and I felt tears starting in my eyes too.

'Isn't Mutti's dress lovely?' I said, my throat aching.

Mags nodded and sniffed, wiping her eyes with her sleeve. 'And that's Mrs Fisher, isn't it?'

'Yes, I think so. She always wore that awful hat.'

'Who's that?' She pointed at the fair-haired man with the little beard.

'No idea — I've never seen him before,' I said. 'A friend of Pa's? A relation we've never met?'

We looked at the picture together for a while.

Then Mags said what we were both thinking: 'There's no other family there.'

'No.'

I looked at my young father's eyes, and I realized that there had always been something sad in them, something haunted, even when he was smiling. He had carried some kind of secret grief around with him every single day — right up until the last time we said goodbye.

'I found it in the cellar,' I said. 'Why do you think they put it down there?'

She shrugged. 'Because it should be a happy picture, but for some reason it feels like a sad one.'

'Yes.' That was what I thought too. I considered how

people always thought of wedding days as such joyful occasions, and how romantic stories always ended with the couple getting married and living happily ever after . . .

'Do you think you'll ever get married, Mags?'

I was expecting some sort of jokey, scoffing response – perhaps even an 'over my dead body' – but instead, my sister shrugged silently and stared out towards the sea through the cave's gloomy grey eyes.

Had I said something wrong? There was a wall between us again.

I got up and tidied away the buttery bits of paper from the sandwiches. When I turned around, I saw that my sister had curled up on her bed and closed her eyes. She must have been very tired. I pulled one of the blankets over her gently and went to sit at the front of the cave, peering out at the world that lay beyond.

I felt close to Pa here, looking out over the wind-glazed waves. He was part of the sea he loved. He was in the water and the wind. I imagined his voice telling us stories of shipwrecks and sea monsters, the legend of the Wyrm and the Stones . . .

I had been feeling guilty about tricking Mrs Baron, but now, in this strange, still moment, I knew that Mags and I had done the right thing. How could we have gone to Wales and left our Pa here? How could we have abandoned our lighthouse? I thought about what Mrs Baron had said – that the Castle could be a target for bombers or saboteurs. Something tugged at my mind like a fish caught on a line. *Saboteurs?* I thought of the dark reflection in the kitchen window, the figure I thought I had seen darting behind the standing stone. What if someone was lurking around the lighthouse, waiting for us to leave so that they could break in? What if they wanted to set fire to the lighthouse, just like the village hall? I imagined it burning down like a giant candle.

And then a terrible thought struck me hard.

I had forgotten to lock the main door to the lighthouse. Mags had reminded me, and I had said I would do it, but I had forgotten.

I thought about Pa's service room full of papers and records, logbooks and shipping charts, and I thought about the telephone with the direct line to the Admiralty. Then I thought about that flashing light I had seen on the north cliff before the bomber crashed – someone had been trying to signal to the enemy . . . And I had left our huge lantern unguarded.

I tried to steady my breathing, looking down at the sea. There was the Wyrm – barely visible beneath the choppy waves and the churned-up sea foam. I could just make it out – a squirming, squid-like sea dragon with the dark shapes of swallowed things lurking in its pale stomach. A cold surge of nausea rolled through my body. The more I thought about it, the more certain I was that someone had been there up amongst the stones, watching me, watching the lighthouse. I tortured myself, imagining the lighthouse being used as a beacon for German bombers. I pictured the white cliffs reduced to a pile of chalky rubble . . . And it would all be my fault.

I had to go back.

I glanced at my sister – fast asleep now. She would be angry if I woke her to say I'd forgotten to lock the lighthouse door after all. If I could just nip back there quickly, she would never even know that I had gone . . .

34

There was no sinister figure lurking near the Castle, and there was no sign of anyone having been inside the lighthouse either. I locked the heavy door and then I went back outside, moving around the wall of the cottage carefully, keeping an eye out for the mysterious dark figure, and for Mrs Baron too. The last thing I wanted was to be caught and sent away all by myself, without Mags. There was no sign of her, though. If she had come looking for us, she must have been and gone already. The only sounds were the cries of sea birds in the heavy sky above, and the gusting of the stormy air.

But then there was another sound. There, entwined delicately about the rushes of the wind, was a high, piercing thread of song. *The Daughters of Stone.*

I went straight to the stone on the left — the stone that was pointed at the top like a diamond, the one that had always been *mine*, ever since I was tiny. The song was stronger here — not louder, just, somehow, stronger — sharper and clearer. I put my hand flat against the stone, and it seemed to vibrate beneath my palm, like the heartbeat of an alarmed animal. It felt like a warning.

I thought then about that long, lonely night I had spent on the clifftop, and of how the stones and I had sung to the sea in the eerie dawn light, praying for my father and sister to come safely home. I had made a solemn promise, just as the Daughters had so many centuries before. Pa had been killed, but, miraculously, Mags had come home to me. What did that mean? Was there a price to be paid or not? Would I end up being turned to stone?

Mags would have dismissed the idea as superstitious nonsense. She would have laughed. But I knew that the magic was real. Was it faith, or fear? — that terrible, quiet knowledge I had possessed deep in my bones ever since I had first heard the legend: my fate was somehow entangled with the Wyrm and the stones, and there was nothing that could be done about it.

In that moment, a herring gull landed on top of the stone. I noticed that its beak and eyes were exactly the same shade of vivid yellow as the nose of the German fighter plane. The gull looked right at me with its cold, yellow eyes, opened its beak and let out a piercing peal of screams before flapping its wings and launching itself out over the sea.

The dark clouds were right above me now. The song of the stones seemed to have faded away, or was it just lost amongst the fierce gusts of wind? I pulled my coat closed, doing up the buttons with cold fingers. I fished around in the pockets, hoping I might find a scarf or something in there, but my fingers closed around a crumpled piece of paper instead. *A shopping list?* No. I knew exactly what it was. It was the piece of paper Mags had taken when we were spying on Spooky Joe. In the chaos and grief of those last few weeks, I had forgotten all about it. I smoothed it out and looked again at the mysterious letters and numbers.

MB–TB
0617 040540
0638 110540
0557 180540
0625 250540

I had wondered if the MB had referred to my sister – Magda Bernadette. There was definitely *something* that she wasn't telling me, but if she didn't want to talk to me about it, how could I possibly find out what was going on?

I made up my mind. I would have to be bolder, more direct. I would make my sister tell me the truth.

35

I was on my way back towards the cliff path when I saw a man — a figure on the hill inland — walking right through the middle of one of Mr White's fields, heading away from the Castle. He was wearing a dark coat and hat. At first I thought it was Mr White himself, but then I saw that the figure was taller, leaner, and his stride was swift and athletic. It wasn't the farmer at all — it looked more like Michael Baron . . .

It *was* Michael Baron.

What was *he* doing up here? More to the point, what was he doing in the middle of Mr White's pea field? There was something odd and unsettling about the scene. Was it to do with the way Michael was walking? The pea plants were a sea of green under the grey storm-light — the colour of veins on a white wrist.

They rippled like pond-water as he strode through them.

I couldn't let Michael Baron see me – he might tell his mother I was there. It was possible she had even sent him to look for us. I was about to make a dash for it down the cliff path when he did something that made me stop and crouch behind the bramble bush that bordered the field.

He was now running through the plants to the edge of the field. He stopped at the telegraph pole that carried the telephone wire up to the Castle from the Dover Road and then looked back over his shoulder. As I watched, he shinned up the first few feet of the pole, and then clambered quickly all the way to the top, like a sailor monkeying his way up to the crow's nest.

What is he doing? My hands gripped the bramble branches in front of me, the thorns pricking my fingers. When he reached the top of the pole, he took something out of his pocket and reached up towards the wire. The black cable suddenly dropped – it swung down like a trapeze wire, and was lost in the hedgerow.

Michael Baron had cut the telephone line.

It felt as if the cliffs were trembling beneath my feet, but then I realized that it wasn't the ground that was shaking – it was me.

This wasn't real life at all – how could it be? The dull, pewter light made it all the more surreal: clouds filled the whole sky now – brooding above me.

Michael Baron made his way down the telegraph pole and starting striding back across the field. *He's coming this way*, I thought, but there wasn't time for me to run to the cottage or the lighthouse – he would see me. The only thing I could do was hide myself more deeply in the hedge. I tucked down into a ball and burrowed backwards, ignoring the thorns digging into my back and neck. My folded-up legs were still shaking and I had to put my scratched hands flat on the ground to stop myself from toppling over. I couldn't see anything now except the patch of ground in front of me. I heard Michael approaching. A gull screamed overhead. There was a scuffling noise and then a thud as Michael climbed over the fence and jumped down just a few feet away from me. Then I heard his footsteps making for the path leading to the south cliff.

I followed him.

Looking back, it was such a stupid thing to do. I should have gone straight to the police station and told them what I had just seen: an act of sabotage. And what exactly did that make our headmistress's handsome son? A collaborator, a fifth columnist? These were words I had heard on the wireless or seen in the news-paper, but they were suddenly as real as the rock beneath my feet. This was an act that could only help the enemy. What else had he done? And where was he going now?

Michael covered the ground quickly – he was tall, so his paces were much longer than mine. At points I had to trot to keep him in sight, ducking behind bushes from time to time in case he turned around. When we reached the barbed wire near Spooky Joe's cottage, I stopped and stared. I could still see the neatly snipped ends where Michael had cut Mags free. How stupid I had been! Why would anyone go wandering over the clifftops so early in the morning with a pair of wire cutters in their pocket unless they were up to no good? Yet we hadn't suspected a thing! I turned around, scanning the path and the clifftop for Michael's figure, but he had completely vanished from sight.

Up there on the south cliff, there were only two ways he could have vanished so quickly, and it was pretty unlikely that Michael Baron had spontaneously thrown himself off the cliff . . . So that left only one option. He must have taken the tunnel.

Mags.

It was then that I realized I must have left the torch at the Castle when I went back to lock the door. I had never been up or down the tunnel without one. Under these circumstances – completely alone, chasing a criminal whom I knew to be armed with a sharp tool – bathed in the odd light of the gathering clouds, I was frankly surprised that I was still managing to put one foot in front of the other. I approached the old lookout tower and the entrance to the tunnel. I squatted down. 'You'd better be grateful for this, Mags,' I whispered under my breath. 'I might be about to save your life.' Then I launched myself into the darkness.

It was terrifying. A hellish helter-skelter through absolute darkness, like falling through a nightmare – squeezing and twisting, then slipping blindly while unknown things scratched my face and tore at my hair – down, down, down I fell, deeper into the earth. I may have been the one chasing, rather than being chased, but that didn't make me feel any less like a helpless creature, like something's prey. My feet and hands felt the change from loose soil to smooth chalk as I skidded from the upper burrow into the carved-out passage below. I slithered down a steep slope and the blackness was suddenly diluted into a dull, grey haze. The cave at last.

There was no sign of Michael, but my sister was awake and sitting up at the very front of the cave, staring out through the skull's left eyehole.

'Mags!' I panted. 'Are you all right?'

'I'm fine, Petra – where on earth have you been?'

'I had to go back to the lighthouse.'

'Why—?'

'It doesn't matter now. Mags – did Michael Baron come through here?'

She stared at me.

'Michael Baron – have you seen him? I've just

followed him from the lighthouse. He *must* have come down here. Mags – he's the saboteur!'

She blinked. 'You're insane, Petra,' she said, after a stunned pause.

'Mags! I'm serious – remember the wire cutters he had when he helped free you from the barbed wire? I just watched him use those to cut the telephone line to the Castle!'

'*What?* Why would he want to do that?'

'I don't know, Mags! To cut off the line to the Admiralty, I suppose – to buy time if German U-boats or landing craft are spotted from the lighthouse? It could be lots of different things, but it's not exactly going to be for a *nice* reason, is it?' Then something else occurred to me – a flash of light. 'MB!' I said.

'*What?*'

'Look!' I found the scrap of paper in my coat pocket and thrust it in front of her face. 'This is what Spooky Joe was writing down that morning when we were spying on him.'

Mags frowned. 'I thought I'd lost—'

'Well, I found it again,' I interrupted. 'I don't know what all the numbers mean yet but look, here at the top – MB – Michael Baron!'

'MB could stand for anything, you idiot,' Mags spat. 'It could stand for . . . motor boat or moon beam or . . . mountain bear!'

It was my turn to blink at her. 'Why would anyone

be making secret notes about mountain bears, Mags? At first I thought it might even have been you – Magda Bernadette – but then when I saw Michael—'

'You thought *what*?'

'Please, Mags, listen! It *must* be Michael – it all fits together, don't you see? He's the one behind the sabotage, Mags. I bet it was him that cut the other telephone lines and set the village hall on fire too!'

'You're *wrong*, Petra,' Mags said, her voice trembling with rage.

Why wouldn't she listen to me?

'I've got to go straight to the police station,' I said. 'Come with me, Mags – please.'

She shook her head. She looked frightened, furious. 'You're being ridiculous,' she said. 'I don't believe a word of it. You need to stay here where you are safe, Petra. The whole point of coming to the cave was to protect us from being sent away. If you go to the police . . .'

'This is more important than that, Mags. Can't you see? This is about the war, the *invasion*!'

I saw that her hands were shaking. What was wrong with her? What had happened to my sister – the fearless girl who fought the bullies, the hero who had sailed over to Dunkirk and saved the lives of our stranded soldiers? Through the eyeholes in the rock behind her, I could see dark storm clouds swelling and gathering fast. My sister's eyes were just as angry.

'It's *not* about the invasion,' she snapped. 'It's about you being a ridiculous child with too much imagination. Don't you *dare* go to the police with these stories about Michael.'

In that one unguarded moment, I saw a flash of truth on her face. I took a step back from her, towards the lower section of the tunnel.

'He *was* here, wasn't he, Mags? Michael *did* come through here! Why are you lying to me? You've been lying to me for months – to all of us! You have to tell me now, Mags – what's going on?'

It was no use. Her jaw was locked with obstinate rage and her eyes were the same as the volcanic-grey irises that gloomed behind her head.

I took another step back from her.

'I said, *stay here*, Petra,' she growled.

But I didn't.

36

The constable on duty at the desk was the same one who had come to search the lighthouse after Mutti's tribunal – the one with the oily moustache.

'I need to report an act of sabotage,' I said, as soon as I got through the door. I leant over the desk towards the policeman, breathing hard. 'The telephone line to the lighthouse has been cut.'

Oily looked at me. He made a note of what I had just said. 'And when did this happen, miss?' he asked.

'About half an hour ago. It's very important,' I said. 'It's not just a normal telephone line, it was installed by the Admiralty, for emergencies.'

Oily made a note of that too. 'Did you see this happen?'

'Yes, I did. And I saw who did it too – it was Michael Baron.'

He put his pen down. 'Michael Baron, the magistrate's son?'

'Yes.'

'Are you sure?'

'Yes.'

Oily looked at me very closely. 'You live at the lighthouse, don't you? One of the half-German girls. Your mum was locked up for being a traitor.'

I looked at him hard. 'No, she was interned for being an enemy alien. It's a very different thing.'

'And it was Mrs Baron who locked her up, wasn't it?'

'Yes,' I said, 'Mrs Baron was one of the magistrates at the tribunal, but what's that got to do with—'

'It's just a bit of a coincidence, that's all,' Oily interrupted. 'Seems to me that you might want to cause trouble for her – to get your own back or something.'

'No!' I said. 'I'm telling the truth! You have to tell Pinstripe – the detective, I mean. I don't know his name – the one in the pinstriped suit. You have to tell him about it right away.' I fished the scrap of paper from my pocket. 'Give him this, please. It's vital evidence – look, *MB*!'

Oily's face was a pantomime of confusion. He shook his head. 'Not sure I know who you mean by *Pinstripe*, miss, but I'll pass on your "evidence" if you really want me to.' He took the scrap of paper from me and put it on the desk without even looking at it, then he slicked down his moustache with a greasy thumb and forefinger. 'But it would be more than my job's worth to cause problems for the local magistrate. I'm sure you understand. I'm hardly going to risk my position on the word of a spiteful child.' He looked me up and down – my coat was covered with mud and chalk from the tunnel. 'And a scruffy little devil at that. I think you'd better run along home, don't you?' He stood up. 'And you can take your tall tales with you.'

I made my way to the cliff path, wary of being seen by Mrs Baron or anyone else in the village who knew that I was supposed to have been evacuated that afternoon.

I drove my fists down into my pockets and fought back the angry tears. The policeman hadn't believed me. My own *sister* hadn't believed me. She had taken Michael's side – the side of a *traitor*. My feet moved heavily up the hill, weighed down by feelings of misery and betrayal and fear. Fat raindrops started falling from the rainclouds that blistered the sky above. They spattered on my head and ran down the back of my neck. As I pulled up the collar of my coat, I realized I was going in the wrong direction for the tunnel. Quite instinctively, I was heading home to the Castle. As I trudged up the steepest part of the path and my home gradually emerged from the rainy haze, something else occurred to me: perhaps when I thought I had seen a dark figure reflected in the kitchen window that afternoon, it hadn't been my imagination playing tricks on me after all. Perhaps it had been *him* lurking around the lighthouse, hiding behind the standing stones. 'Yes,' I breathed. 'Michael Baron.'

And then I froze. It was as if I had summoned him, like some sort of medieval demon, just by speaking his name.

'Hello, Petra.'

37

His voice was behind me.

I turned. Michael Baron was standing on the path that led from the south cliff. A shaft of cold, white sunlight shot down through a crack in the storm clouds directly behind him so that I was looking up at his tall, grim silhouette. He was in the same dark coat and hat that he had been wearing when I saw him in the pea field, but now his clothes were smeared with dirt and chalk, just like mine. He had definitely been through the tunnel.

'You're supposed to be on your way to the wilds of Wales right now, aren't you, Pet?'

I stepped backwards as he came closer.

'I saw what you did, Michael,' I said. 'I saw you cut

the telephone line.'

'Ah. I did wonder. I noticed that you were following me across the cliff. About as subtle as a purple elephant. You'd be a rubbish spy.'

'It was sabotage.'

He smiled. His green eyes had never looked so cruel. '*Sabotage* is a pretty stupid word to band about if you don't actually understand what's going on.'

'I know perfectly well what's going on.'

'Do you? Hitler's army will be here any day now. There is nothing we can do to stop him, and why would we even want to? It will be a glorious new beginning for England.'

I can only imagine that my face looked as baffled as my brain was at that moment.

'My father always said that this country desperately needs a ruler like Hitler – someone to bring back the discipline and wealth of the old Empire. "Just look at the German economy!" Father used to say. So I looked, and eventually I understood. It's about being strong. Unsentimental.

'All that rubbish the vicar was spouting in church about good and evil – as if the real world is that black and white! You're cleverer than that, aren't you, Pet? You can see the true way forward.' He took another step towards me.

I stood my ground. 'You cut the other phone lines too, and started the fires in the village, didn't you?' I had to know that it was him.

'Necessary steps, I'm afraid. It's just about removing obstacles . . .'

'But why the Scout hut?' I didn't understand.

'The LDV were stashing weapons there — shotguns and rifles. We couldn't risk them being used when Hitler's army arrives. Anyway — I'm pretty sure our own police wouldn't have been too happy if they'd found out about it. You can't have people like *that* taking the law into their own hands.'

'But it's all right for people like you?'

'Oh, little Pet,' Michael said, and a muscle twitched in his handsome jaw. 'I'm getting rather bored of this. You clearly don't have a clue what you're talking about.'

His withering tone made me feel I was being ridiculous — childish and ignorant and ridiculous. But then I thought about my Mutti and the Rossis and all the terrible things that were happening at that very moment to innocent people all over Europe. I wasn't clever enough to argue with Michael — I didn't know anything about economies or empires — but I knew that his words made me feel sick. They stank.

'The police know all about you,' I said. 'I told them you cut the telephone line.' I didn't mention the fact that the stupid oily policeman had refused to believe a word of it. 'They're probably coming for you right now.'

'You're bluffing,' he said, and he took another step closer. 'Anyway, even if you have told the police, you haven't got any proof. It's just your word against mine, and who's going to believe a scruffy little orphan over the son of the local magistrate?'

'I'm *not* an orphan,' I shouted. I couldn't stop myself – he was even closer now and I shoved him backwards.

Michael stumbled very slightly, and then laughed. 'I'm disappointed in you, Pet.' His voice had become oddly light and playful. 'You're trying to ruin my beautiful plan, aren't you?' Then, before I knew what was happening, he had grabbed me by the wrist. I yelped with pain, squirming as his hand crushed my bones.

'Let go of me!' I screamed.

'Just your word against mine, Pet,' he said again. 'And if you can't talk to the police because you've *disappeared*, so much the better.' He twisted my arm around, forcing me off the path towards the crumbling edge of the cliff. My shoes skidded helplessly on the wet ground. One foot shot forwards, sending a shower of soil and chalk down into the dark, crashing waves hundreds of feet below. I scrambled frantically, tearing up handfuls of wet turf with my free hand. 'Michael, please – let me go!' He crouched behind me, careful not to get too close to the edge himself, then he twisted my arm again – and forced me, sliding and screaming, towards the cliff edge. All I could think about in that terrifying moment was the childhood game I used to play with Mags on the standing stones – when my sister would slash with her toy sword at the tentacles of sea monsters to set me free from their twisting grasp. But my big sister wasn't here now.

'Let GO!' With my free hand, I grabbed a big lump of chalk, twisted around, and dashed it into Michael's face as he crouched behind me. The chalk was fossil-dry and it exploded as it slammed into his forehead, stunning him. The seconds melted together strangely then, like a gramophone record being played at the wrong speed. Familiar sounds seemed to be bleeding through the air – a thin wailing from the village below, the growl of engines in the sky above. I felt Michael's grip on my wrist loosen, and he toppled on to his back, swearing. I hauled myself back up on to the grass, away from the edge, pushing my toes into the damp ground, and I ran – up on to the clifftop, towards the Castle and the Daughters of Stone.

Michael wasn't far behind me. My legs were burning and I thought my chest would burst, but somehow I kept running. For once in my life the ghastly, searing terror didn't freeze me, it propelled me forwards – I knew that with one great stride, Michael would be on my heels, able to reach forward and grab a fistful of my hair. So many awful sounds filled the air – the thumping of Michael's feet, the blasting of the rain-soaked wind, the deafening sound of engines ripping through the sky above, the sharp cracking of the anti-aircraft guns up on the south cliff; and then, as I drew closer to them, the song of the Daughters of Stone. They were calling to me more clearly – more urgently – than ever before. They loomed before me like tombstones. An aeroplane roared above us. Then there was a different sound altogether – shrill and insistent and dangerous and getting louder by the second. I knew exactly what it was. I threw myself to the ground just as the bomb pounded into the clifftop. The whole world went white, then black, and I was aware of the sensation of moving against my will – up at first, up through the air, and then the ground falling away beneath me and everything suddenly rushing down, down . . .

38

I am falling through the air in a thousand broken pieces. I am the wreckage of a person, I am rubble. I am exactly the same as the vast chunk of chalk that is falling with me — the universe does not know the difference between us, and it does not care. The chalk and I are falling at the same speed, and soon we will both smash and shatter into bone-white dust.

Everything is quiet now.

Perhaps it is a dream, I think, but I know that it is real. Everything that just happened was real. A moment ago, the world exploded, and the white cliffs fell.

The hostile engines in the sky above have roared away over the water, vanishing into the smoke.

I am still falling, and I think perhaps it would be best if I could keep falling for ever. But then comes the unbearable jolt

252

as my body slams into the ground . . . There is no pain. I am
surprised that there is no pain. There is nothing but darkness
and the song of the stones. But something feels strange.
Different. Because now the song is coming from deep within
my own body.

And I know that I am part of the legend at last.

When I opened my eyes, it was to the dark-pink light
of dawn. I was lying on the damp turf of the clifftop.
The song of the Daughters of Stone was like a needle
piercing through my nightmares, a beautiful bee sting.
My head was turned towards the sea, and the first rays
of sunlight burst like a thousand golden stars from the
glowing horizon. It was the most glorious thing I had
ever seen.

I felt very cold, but I was aware of someone moving
around close to me. They seemed to be untying something from my shoulders and putting a blanket over my
body, gently tucking it in around me. They were whis-
pering soothing words. I tried to turn my head to see,
but it hurt too much.

'Pa?' I said. My voice was a sleepy growl.

And then there was a face – a deeply lined face, with
bright blue eyes and white hair that blew wildly about
in the breeze.

'It's me, Petra. It's Joe.'

Spooky Joe? I didn't understand. 'How . . .'

'It doesn't matter now. I came looking for you and

your sister after the air raid.'

The air raid. Yes.

'I fell,' I muttered, aware that my voice sounded far away. There was dust in my throat, and my body felt very strange, but I couldn't work out why. 'There was a bomb.' I coughed, and icicles of pain stabbed through my chest, neck and shoulders.

'Yes,' said Joe. 'There was a bomb, Petra. It just missed the lighthouse. It blew away a chunk of the cliff, and you fell on to a ledge below. I climbed down and brought you back up. You've been unconscious all night. I've just been back to the Castle to fetch blankets and I tried to call for an ambulance but the telephone was dead.'

The telephone was dead. Michael Baron. He had been there on the clifftop. What had happened to him?

'Was there anyone else? When you found me?'

'No. No one else. Was your sister with you?'

'Mags. No. She's still in the cave.'

'Dragon Bay Cave? In the tunnel?'

'Yes.'

'I'll go and get her.'

But he didn't need to. I could hear her voice.

'Petra? PET!'

'She's all right,' Joe called to her. 'She's all right, Magda.'

My sister was running. I could feel the thudding of her feet, hear her breaths getting closer. And then she was on her knees beside me, cradling my face, and she was crying.

'Pet – I'm so sorry – are you all right? Are you really all right?'

I tried to turn towards her but for some reason I couldn't move. I suddenly realized what it was about my body that felt so very, very wrong.

'Mags,' I whispered, trying to keep the terror from my voice.

My sister took my hand. 'What is it, Pet?'

'Mags. I can't feel my legs.'

'She needs an ambulance,' Joe said in a low voice. 'As soon as possible. Can you run down to the village? You'll be quicker than me.'

'Yes,' my sister breathed. 'Yes, of course.' She kissed me on the forehead and I felt her tears wet against my skin and hair. 'I'll be back before you know it, Pet.'

And she was gone again.

I lay there, staring up into the flaming ribbons of cloud above, trying hard to remember everything that had happened the evening before: Michael cutting the telephone line, the argument with Magda, the police station, the chase across the clifftop, the bomb, falling through the air . . .

After a while I started to feel very, very tired. My eyes closed against the brightening sunlight.

'Stay awake,' Joe said.

Thoughts swirled sleepily in my mind like honey in

hot milk. The song of the stones was a lullaby now.

I could feel Joe's hand on my arm. 'Stay awake, Pet. Listen to me. Open your eyes.'

I opened them and tried to make his face come into focus. A strange thought swam into my head.

'You know about Dragon Bay Cave, Joe,' I whispered. 'You know the tunnel?'

'Know about it?' He smiled then – and it was something wonderful. His eyes lit up, bright blue. 'I dug it.'

I didn't understand – Joe had only moved to the village last summer.

'How do you think I got down to the beach so quickly when that German bomber came down?'

'But . . .'

'Don't worry about it now, Petra.'

'And the telephone – I locked the lighthouse . . .'

'I'll explain,' he said. 'I'll explain everything.'

Then there were voices coming closer. My sister had brought half of the village with her. Mrs Baron was there, and Edie from the bakery, and several policemen too – though it didn't look like the oily one was with them.

'The ambulance is on its way,' Mags said.

I could hear Mrs Baron's voice: 'You should have gone! You should both have been on that wretched bus. I said it was too dangerous for you to stay here – if you'd gone, none of this would have happened!' She sounded angry, and terribly anxious, close to tears.

My sister's voice was quieter. She was kneeling beside me again. 'I should have been with you, Pet. I shouldn't have let you go alone. I'm so sorry.'

'It's all right, Mags,' I managed to say.

Edie gave me a sip of water.

Mrs Baron was talking to the policemen.

'Michael, my son, Michael – he hasn't been home since the air raid . . .'

'He was here,' I whispered.

'What? What did she say?' And everyone was suddenly quiet. Mrs Baron bent down towards me. 'Michael was here?'

One of the policemen bent down too. 'During the air raid? Are you sure, miss? He was up here on the cliff when the bomb fell?'

'Yes.'

Mrs Baron's face was white, stricken. Both her hands were pressed flat to her heart. Mags had gone pale too. They were both looking at the policemen, who had retreated a few paces away and were talking to each other quietly.

'It doesn't look good . . .'

'A search party . . .'

'Check the beach under the cliffs, we'll need to go through the rock-fall . . .'

Then Mags's voice: 'I'm sure it's all right, Mrs Baron,' she said, standing up. 'I'm sure he'll be all right. I'll help search.'

'Thank you.' Mrs Baron looked genuinely grateful. 'We'll search together, Magda.'

'Did you say the girls should have been evacuated yesterday, Mrs Baron?' one of the policemen asked then.

'What? Yes,' she said, distracted. She could only think of Michael now.

'I was just going to suggest that I could contact the authorities on your behalf so you don't have to worry . . .'

But another voice cut the policeman off. 'There'll be no need for that,' Joe said very steadily. 'I'll be looking after them both now. I'll take care of my granddaughters.'

39

Spooky Joe was our grandfather. He was Pa's dad.
In the ambulance on the way to the hospital,
he just sat beside me very quietly, his hand on
my arm. My thoughts were blurred and strange, but I
was dimly aware that a few pieces of the puzzle were
falling into place at last: his piercing blue eyes and
familiar, square shoulders; the fact that I had mistaken
his silhouette for Pa's in the rowing boat that night; his
face when I called the *King Edward* 'our boat' (*he* had
built the boat for my Pa when Pa was just a boy). I
remembered seeing Pa wave to Joe on the morning the
German bomber crashed into the cabbage field, and it
had been clear that Mutti knew who he was too,
though she had refused to tell me when I'd asked.

I thought sleepily about all the children I knew who

had grown up with their cuddly grans, who gave them pennies for sweets, and their kind old grandpops, who took them to play cricket on the beach. And I thought how odd it was that I had never even thought to ask Pa about his parents. I had always just accepted that it was only the four of us. Why had they never told us about him? Why hadn't they spoken to him since he moved back to Stonegate?

It was a few days later that I found out the answers.

I woke up from a long deep sleep to find Joe sitting beside my hospital bed. I tried to sit up and roll towards him, but then remembered – for what felt like the hundredth time already – that my legs didn't seem to be working properly. I turned my head instead, the hospital sheet cool and crisp against my neck and cheek.

'Hello, Spooky Joe,' I said.

His eyes twinkled. 'That's Grandpa Joe to you, young lady. How are you feeling?'

'All right, thank you. Less bruised than yesterday.'

'Your legs?'

I shook my head. 'Still nothing.'

He nodded, swallowed hard, and looked towards the window, which was pink with geraniums.

'Joe,' I said, 'tell me about the tunnel. You said you dug it. You said you'd explain . . .'

'I did, didn't I?' He took a long breath. 'Well, I didn't exactly dig the tunnel, if I'm honest – I re-dug it,' he admitted. 'The main shaft was dug out by smugglers hundreds of years ago, but most of the top section had collapsed. My brother Charlie and I dug it out again.' He paused. 'When we was about your age, I reckon. Feels like lifetimes ago.'

'Your brother?'

I thought his eyes became glassy then. He leant forward, pressed my hand between his, and took another deep breath. 'We went off to the war together, Charlie and me. The Great War, I mean, of course – not this one. Poor Charlie got killed. I haven't . . . I've never talked about it. I can't bear to think about the things that happened. The things I saw.'

I felt that I could almost see the shadows of memories in his eyes.

'But I need to tell you this, I think, Pet.' He waited for a moment, and then he said, 'It was in the war – in the trenches. My brother went out into no man's land to help a lad who'd got hit by shrapnel the day before. We could hear him out there, crying with the pain. He was frightened, calling for his mum.' Joe shook his head, as if to shake the sound from his mind. 'We'd listened to him all through that night and Charlie couldn't take it any longer. He got up at dawn and just said, "I'm going to get him. I'm going to bring him back here to the trench, and if I can't, I'll just have to put a bullet in the poor boy's brain." We couldn't stop him.'

He paused as if trying to decide if he could continue. He swallowed. 'The boy was very badly hurt and all caught up in barbed wire too. Charlie tried to untangle him and then . . .' Joe breathed heavily. Once, twice. 'Then the machine guns started. Charlie held up his hands to show he was unarmed – he was just collecting a casualty. But they blew him to bits. Charlie and the other injured boy – just blew them to bits on the barbed wire.'

Oh, God. 'Poor Charlie,' I breathed.

'Yes.'

I squeezed Joe's old hand.

'I'm sorry, Pet,' Joe said. 'It's horrible to hear, I know.'

I had never heard anyone speak about the last war like this. It had always seemed sealed up, closed over, like a scarred wound.

'But you need to know what happened to Charlie to understand why . . . why things went so wrong between me and your Pa.'

I looked at him. His eyes were so like my Pa's – round and ocean-blue – and full of sad, sad stories. I thought of the wedding photograph and suddenly I understood.

'Mutti?' I whispered.

'Yes. Your mother.' He looked down at the floor. 'We couldn't accept it – your grandmother and I. We couldn't understand how our son could fall in love with a German girl, not after that war, after

Charlie . . . My wife was very ill by then and the news that they were getting married was the end of her. Your Pa and I haven't spoken since the day of her funeral. I moved away just after.'

I thought of Pa and Mutti's lonely wedding day; the solemn, haunted faces of the bride and groom. My grandmother, Pa's mother, had died just before he married Mutti, and Joe had always blamed them for her death.

'And time goes by, doesn't it? It's frightening how quickly time goes by.' Joe's eyes were brimming with tears now. His gnarled hand clasped mine.

All those lost years . . .

'I came back to try to build a bridge with your Pa, but then this war started, and . . . everything just came flooding back again.'

I thought about him calling Mutti 'Jerry' in Mrs Rossi's bakery. Joe had come back to Stonegate to try to put the past behind him, but he had not been able to, and Pa had died before the rift could be mended.

'I spent so long hating what I thought was the enemy,' he whispered hoarsely, 'but I was wrong. Time is the greatest enemy of all.' He looked right into my eyes then, and for a moment it was as if Pa were there with me. 'Every bit of hate left me the moment I saw that lump blown out of the cliff and you all crumpled up on the ledge below. I thought I'd lost you as well as your Pa.'

He looked terribly lost then, terribly alone.

I wanted to put my arms around him, but I couldn't sit up.

'Our Mutti didn't kill your brother, Grandpa Joe,' I said. I tried to swallow the rough, painful lump in my throat. 'Our Mutti is the most gentle person in the whole world.'

Joe sobbed once and tears spilt down his weather-worn cheeks. He squeezed my hand more tightly between his. 'I'm sure she is, Petra,' he said.

I heard the faint calls of seagulls from somewhere beyond the window.

'And she does beautiful paintings – of the sea, and the cliffs and the lighthouse. I think you would like her.'

Joe wiped his eyes. He nodded, trying to smile. 'I . . . I've never actually spoken to her.'

'You will,' I said, and I was surprised by the strength and certainty that was there in my voice. 'You will, Grandpa Joe.'

40

I t was later that afternoon that the doctor came to tell me the bad news.

'It's broken, Miss Smith,' he said. 'Your back. Broken in two different places, we think.'

I was falling through the air again with the chalk dust and the chunk of clifftop. Once more I felt the jolt as my body slammed into the ledge below. Broken. Broken in two places. There was only darkness – darkness and the song of the stones.

'Will it heal?' My voice sounded much braver and calmer than I felt inside.

'The back itself will heal with time,' he said. 'But we don't know yet about the nerves in your spine that are responsible for the feeling and movement in your legs. It may be that the nerves are just bruised.' His expression changed then. 'But it's quite possible, Miss Smith, that they may never fully recover. It's possible, I'm afraid, that you might never walk again.'

This had been my nightmare all my life, both sleeping and awake: to be frozen. Paralysed. Petrified. But this was not how I had expected it to happen. And there was something else unexpected too: I did not feel as helpless as I had thought I would. Do you know what the name Petra means? I can tell you now if you don't know. It means rock. Stone.

I was a Daughter of Stone now.

And stone is strong.

The hospital was clean and comfortable, and the nurses were cheerful, but I had never been away from home before, and it wasn't long before I started pining for the big skies of Stonegate and the bright sea air. It didn't seem to matter that I couldn't move about on my own – here in the hospital, inland, I was a fish out of water anyway. Every now and then I would hear the distant calls of gulls through the open windows and it made me ache even more than my bruises did.

I was allowed to return home a few weeks later, strapped into a heavy back brace. Grandpa Joe collected me and took me home in a taxi. He had arranged with the coastguard to take up his old job as lighthouse keeper again, so that he could look after me and my sister and we wouldn't have to be evacuated.

Mags made a sponge cake to welcome me back and Grandpa Joe bought me a beautiful new sketchbook and set of pencils. Every morning, he carried me up to the lantern room so that I could sit and watch the sea and draw the things I saw through the windows, and the things I saw in my mind too. I drew my whole story – from Mags's black eye on the first day of the war through to the pink geraniums in the hospital window boxes. And while I sat up there, sketching and shading, bathed in summer light, the war continued – and so did life in the rest of the Castle. Barnaby still hunted rabbits every morning and dozed on my lap in the afternoons, but some other things had changed a great deal.

Mags was now a paler, quieter version of the heroic big sister I used to know. She volunteered with the lifeboat crew, and when she wasn't working down at the harbour, she was out walking across the cliffs all by herself. She became dreadfully thin. When I looked at her I thought of the word *dwindled* – yes, that's the word – dwindled. Like a dying fire. And it was all because of Michael Baron.

They had searched for Michael for days after the bombing. The police concluded that his body must have fallen all the way down to the beach below, and been swept away with the tide. Mrs Baron's hair turned as grey as sea spray, and her eyes were no longer as bright as a kestrel's. They were red and small, and seemed to have sunk deep into her skull.

The inquest returned the verdict of accidental death and there was a memorial for Michael in the church. Nothing was ever said about my accusation of sabotage, and I never told a soul what had happened before the air raid – Michael's zealous speech about Hitler, and how he had tried to push me over the edge of the cliff . . . Now that he was dead, I thought it might be best to keep these awful things to myself. It wasn't like keeping Pa's secret, though – to protect his memory. This was different. This was to protect Mags.

We had never spoken about it, but I knew why Mags had lied about Michael having been there in Dragon Bay Cave after he cut the phone line, why she didn't want to believe that he was a saboteur, why she wouldn't come to the police station, why she was so angry with me, and why she was desperate not to be evacuated.

'You loved him, didn't you?' I said, when I saw her all dressed up for his memorial, a layer of Mutti's pancake make-up covering the purple hollows beneath her eyes.

She looked at me for a moment, and then she nodded.

'Yes.'

She and Michael had been meeting for months – up on the cliffs or down in Dragon Bay Cave. I remembered that misty morning when I had followed Mutti and discovered that Mutti was following someone else. She had been following Mags after all. She knew Mags was meeting someone.

'But why didn't you say anything, Mags? Why did it all have to be so secret?'

She just shook her head. 'I can't explain, Pet.'

I helped her put her hat on, pinning it carefully and tucking the curls around her ears.

'Do you want me to come with you?' I said. 'You can push me in the wheelchair.' But she shook her head again. And she went to the memorial alone.

One of the dreadful things about war is that it doesn't pause to let you catch your breath. There is no time to grieve. It rattles on, like a monstrous juggernaut. Within the space of a few months, Mutti had been taken away, Pa had died, the bomb had fallen, Michael had been killed, and now my sister was disappearing in front of my eyes.

People said that if the invasion was coming at all, it would be very soon. I was a Daughter of Stone now – so, from up in the lantern room, from first light to twilight, I did what the Daughters of Stone do: I kept watch over our sky and sea. The weeks of summer went by and faded to autumn. There were flames in the sky nearly every day – flames and smoke and explosions and bullets like blazing rain and the furious battling of our planes against theirs. There were days when I watched from dawn, when the sea was still, misty and milky white, through the rolling blue of the morning, to the tufted waves and mackerel skies of midday. I watched the colours of the sea and the sky shifting together, like a beautiful dance of light. I saw all of this, and I thought about my poor lost Pa. I worried about my sister, drifting around the Castle and the clifftops as insubstantial as sea mist – as if the heart had been torn out of her. I thought about my Mutti far away from us, locked up in her internment camp. And I thought about the Rossis, and all the others who had been taken too.

A very sad thing happened to Mr Miller – the elderly German man who had been so kind and hopeful on the day of Mutti's tribunal.

Despite being classed as Category C enemy aliens, he and his wife were eventually put in an internment camp anyway. Then Mr Miller was separated from his wife and was sent to Canada on a ship called the *Arandora Star*. The ship was sunk by a German U-boat and he drowned. Over eight hundred people drowned. I can't say how many of those people were on the side of the Nazis – I expect some of them must have been, but everyone knew that Mr Miller was the sweetest, most harmless old man in the world, and there must have been others like him on the ship too: innocent people. The Millers had come to England for a new life because their home was not safe for them any more.

'This is a good country,' Mr Miller had said to my Mutti. 'A free country. They will see the truth in you.'

Grandpa Joe just shook his head when we heard about the *Arandora Star* on the wireless. His blue eyes swam with tears.

41

October was a cold, dark month and Hallowe'en was the coldest, darkest day of all – one of those very cruel autumn days that feel like a dress rehearsal for winter. All day long, the weather crouched over the lighthouse like a giant spider. Grandpa Joe went to Dover – to the magistrate's court. Mrs Baron called by in the morning and asked him to meet her there in the afternoon. She said there were some forms to do with legal guardianship that he had to complete, so he caught the bus just after lunch. I thought how kind it was of her to be sorting things out for us when she must have been grieving terribly for Michael.

Mags baked bread. I sat up in the lantern room and listened to her moving around in the kitchen below, the dough thudding rhythmically into the flour on the kitchen table. Yesterday, she said there was something important she needed to talk to me about, but she wasn't sure if she was quite ready yet, and today it seemed that she could hardly look me in the eye. She had been spending more and more of her time out of the house. I watched her walking over the cliffs — through the rain or fog. I wondered if she went up to the south cliff to feel close to Michael, in the same way that I felt close to Pa when I was looking out to sea.

At last I heard her footsteps coming up towards the lantern room.

'Can I get you anything, Pet? A cup of tea or anything?'

She could have asked me that through the speaking tube.

'I'm fine, thanks, Mags. Is Grandpa Joe still not home?' I knew that he wasn't.

'Not yet.'

She sat down next to me. She was wearing a pale yellow scarf that might once have belonged to Mutti. Her hands were folded in her lap, and that made me think of Mutti too — at the tribunal, her white hands twisted together.

'I need to ask you something, Pet,' she said. 'The day the bomb fell — you said some things about Michael . . .'

We had not discussed it since. I had never told her

that he attacked me, that he was chasing me across the clifftop when the bomb fell. Her heart had been broken enough.

'Were those things true, Pet? Was he really the saboteur?'

What could I say? There are times when the truth can be so much more cruel than a lie. Mags was staring right into my eyes, and I was so close to saying, *Yes, everything I said about Michael was true — and much worse besides*, but then I said, 'It must have been the fall — I can't remember much about that last day. I can't remember what I saw, Mags.'

She looked at me for a moment longer — looked deep into me — then she nodded and turned to stare out of the window. The afternoon sun was a band of rose-gold light beneath the clouds. It shone warmly on her brow, her nose, the strong bones of her cheeks and chin. For a moment, she looked like the sister I remembered.

'I need to go out for a while,' she said.

'It'll get dark soon, Mags.'

'I know, but I shouldn't be too long. And Grandpa Joe will be home any minute.' Then she winked at me. 'Stay right here, Pet.'

I smiled. *Where else could I go?*

An hour or more passed. It was dreadfully lonely up there, and dreadfully cold too. The tide was high but starting to drop now. The shape of the Wyrm twisted beneath the waves like a ghostly serpent. It was hungry. I became aware of a faint, high note buzzing in my chest – the song of the stones – a warning . . . Then, as I looked at the sea, I thought I saw something else – in the deeper water beyond the sandbank. A long, dark shadow. I squinted at it through Pa's telescope but it was no use – it was getting too gloomy to see anything clearly now.

As night closed in on the Castle, it began to rain – heavy drops hammering on the lighthouse roof and strafing the windows – and I wished with all my heart that Grandpa Joe would come home. *What can have happened to him?* There was a dogfight happening several miles out over the sea – I could hear the whining of the engines and the rattle of the guns. Every now and then there were showers of light in the sky – firework-bright. The feeble wail of the village air-raid siren seeped in through the edges of the windows, but I knew that I couldn't get down to the coal cellar by myself.

Perhaps Dover has been bombed, I thought. *Perhaps that's why Grandpa Joe hasn't come home.* But then I shook the thought from my mind. *I can't start thinking like that, not when I am all alone here in the dark – I'll drive myself mad.* I closed my eyes and started counting, promising myself that either Mags or Grandpa Joe would be back by the time I got to one hundred.

But I didn't get to one hundred.

The darkness of the lantern room and the sound of the rain somehow cocooned me. The violence of the world outside was so muffled and so very, very far away . . . My mind slipped sideways into a dream of underwater shadows . . .

There are creatures slithering down here at the bottom of the sea — pale, squirming serpents, fish and eels — disgusting and tortured and suffocating in this liquid darkness. I try to swim away, aware that a huge mass has shifted beneath me — the ocean floor itself, lifting up, stretching out its scaled neck and tail, opening its foul, yawning jaws. It is following me through the black water — my lungs are bursting — I have been holding my breath for a thousand years. I stumble out of the water on to the sand, and I hear its hissing, rasping breath behind me. I scramble away. Its heavy, wet footsteps follow me, its long claws scratch against the rocks. I can feel its rancid breath on my back as it lunges forward, reeking of salt-water corpses and rotting flesh — it has killed so many already — what made me think that I would be the one to outrun it? There is nothing special about me. I fall to my knees, sobbing and panting for breath. I know it will happen now. The bony jaws of the Wyrm are about to close around me and it will all be over . . .

But that moment never came. I was suddenly completely awake, my ears ringing with the noise that had woken me. *Gunfire.*

I looked around in the darkness, my heart still

banging from my nightmare. I strained my eyes to check every inch of the lantern room, listening for noises in the lighthouse and the cottage beneath me, but I knew the answer already. Grandpa Joe had not come back, and neither had Mags.

42

There were planes over the sea, just beyond the cliffs — *four, five of them, maybe* — they were roaring at each other like mechanical dragons, spitting out fire and fury. The world beyond the lantern room was a blurred chaos of smoke and rain and noise.

If I can just fall asleep again, surely the others will be home soon and everything will be fine . . . But I couldn't. Something felt dreadfully wrong. I managed to lift myself up in my chair a little and twist around to look out of the window behind me. Everything was velvet-black — I couldn't even see the outline of the cottage roof — until an explosion in the sky illuminated the world like a ball of lightning, and then I saw something horrible. It was long and pale and yellow and it was lying on the grass just outside the kitchen door. Everything went dark again instantly, but I knew exactly what I had seen. It was the scarf Mags had been wearing earlier. And the door to the kitchen was standing open. And there was something else there too — a lifeless shape slumped on the wet ground.

Mags.

I heard something several floors below and my heart started to thump hard. *Who can it be? Burglars? A saboteur? An enemy parachutist?* What if this was the beginning of the invasion? I couldn't hide. I couldn't do anything. Another flash of fire in the sky outside and I closed my eyes tightly. *What is happening? What has happened to Mags?*

My brain spun through a dark maze of thoughts, and came to its terrible conclusion at exactly the same moment that a noise from the service room made me gasp and open my eyes and turn towards the stairs. *Someone is inside the lighthouse. Mags must have got in their way.* And that same someone was now coming for me.

There was a sound on the stairs — a soft, wet sound, but unmistakeably a footstep, and it was soon followed by another, and then another. Something scraped along the wall as the footsteps ascended the stairs, closer and closer, and I could hear another sound now — the hissing of its breath. I shook my head, struggling to breathe as the familiar terror took hold of my heart and lungs. *It can't be the Wyrm, it can't be* . . . My nightmare had finally come to life – I had conjured it into existence with my dream and my fear. I stared in horror as the shadow of the Wyrm now appeared on the wall in front of me, exactly as I saw it in my nightmare. It was a huge, distorted shape with the unmistakeable long, cruel muzzle of a dragon. It hissed again and I tried to control my panicked breathing, telling myself that I would be waking up soon. *I always wake up at this part, always. I will wake up any second – any second now* . . . But the shadow grew larger, and the hissing of its breath grew louder, and my arms were full of pins and needles. I closed my eyes tightly and waited.

It made its last heavy, wet step up on to the concrete floor of the lantern room, and then there was just the slow hissing of its laboured breath. I pictured it there – scaly and pale and terrible – searching the darkness for me. I could hear the sound of a child sobbing in fear, and it took me a moment to realize that it was me. I thought of Mags, lying on the ground outside and I was nearly sick. *The Wyrm has killed her! Bitten her with its needle-sharp teeth!* I forced myself to open my eyes and saw not a ghastly sea monster at all, but something very different.

It was a slim, dark shape – a human shape – dressed in a long black raincoat and carrying a lantern. Its face was covered with something that in silhouette looked like a dragon's muzzle, something I should have recognized immediately. It was a gas mask. There was another long hiss as the figure drew its breath through the mask. Then it reached up with a black-gloved hand, and pulled the gas mask from its face.

43

Mrs Baron. It was my headmistress, the local magistrate and ARP warden. She was dressed in black from head-to-toe, and she was staring straight at me with her red-rimmed, falcon's eyes. 'It's you,' she said, and she almost laughed, dropping the gas mask on the floor. 'I was worried for a moment that your grandfather had come home. I should have known it was only you. He'll still be stuck in Dover – furious by now that I've sent him on a wild goose chase. He will have been waiting outside my office for hours and hours this afternoon – long enough to miss the last bus home – and then the air-raid sirens will have started . . .' She tutted sarcastically. 'Such unfortunate timing!'

I wrapped my arms tightly around myself, trying to

make sense of what was happening. Mrs Baron had deliberately lured Grandpa Joe away from the Castle so that she could come here – but why?

'I'll put you to sleep in a minute – just like your sister,' Mrs Baron said softly. 'Just a drop of chloroform – it won't do any harm. I was planning on having the two of you evacuated to get you out of the way permanently, but this will have to do for now. It will buy me enough time to finish my work here.'

'Work?' It came out as a croak.

Mrs Baron had found the crank handle for the optic. She fitted it and started turning it with both hands, winding up the mechanism. Her nest of salt-grey hair nodded crazily back and forth. The optic started spinning in the darkness like a ghostly merry-go-round. What was she doing? She couldn't possibly be planning on lighting the lamp – not when there were German planes in the sky.

'It's going to be tonight,' she said, breathless with emotion. 'The invasion! The U-boat will need a bearing to avoid the sandbanks.'

The U-boat? I thought about the shadow I had seen, lurking out there in the water. *Oh, God . . .*

'This bit is particularly important,' she gloated, nodding at the spinning optic. There was a manic spark in her eyes. 'The light has to be flashing to give a positive signal. A steady light is the agreed signal to abandon the landing.' She cackled then. 'When we practised the signal with the Luftwaffe, I had to make do with an oil lamp, up on the clifftop – but *this* lamp! What could be better than this? My husband would have been so proud of me.'

Husband? I remembered Michael talking about his father's vision of the future – the British Empire reborn under a leader like Hitler – and then I was furious with myself: why had I not considered the possibility that Mrs Baron might share the same views? Michael had been brainwashed into his way of thinking by his very own parents.

I have to stop her. I took a deep breath and tried to lift myself up in the chair, but my arms felt almost as numb as my legs. I screwed up my face and willed myself to move, but all I could manage was a feeble wobble before I collapsed into the chair again, air wheezing in and out through my throat, tight with terror.

Mrs Baron laughed. 'What was I worrying about? I won't need to chloroform you at all, will I? You'll be a good girl and stay right there, won't you?' She hummed part of the national anthem, then stopped and laughed again. 'Let's play musical statues, Petra!'

I gritted my teeth and managed to get one of my arms up on to the ledge of the window behind me, but it was no good – the rest of me was rubbery and useless. I couldn't go anywhere. I searched around the room frantically, looking for something I could grab or throw, but there was nothing. The only thing I could see that might possibly help me was just beyond my reach.

Mrs Baron stood back, admiring the optic as it spun soundlessly around. 'And the best thing is that your family will get the blame for this!' she said. 'Who would suspect the ARP warden of operating the lamp in the lighthouse? I'm the one who goes around telling people to put lights *out*!' She took hold of the lever for the lamp and pulled it down hard with both hands. Light exploded out like a white-hot harpoon.

'Mrs Baron!' I shouted, covering my eyes from the sudden glare. 'There are enemy planes out there – you're lighting up the whole coastline for them! They could attack the lighthouse—'

'Tonight's dogfight is just a diversion,' she said coldly, and the light flashed around and around her head like a hellish halo. 'And, anyway, even if we were caught in the crossfire, it would be worth it. I've been waiting so long for tonight. Sacrifices have to be made in wars. Your mother, for example – she was a sacrifice.'

Mutti? And that word 'sacrifice'. For so many years, it had been a word that meant only one thing to me: four girls on a clifftop singing to the sea. Four girls who offered up their lives to save others. In that moment, I was aware of the Daughters of Stone outside on the clifftop, sparkling darkly, calling to me as one of their own – giving me strength. So many lives were at risk now – it wasn't just Mags and my Pa, as it had been at the dawn of Dunkirk. Now it was the harbour, Dover, the white cliffs; it was every soul who lived along our coast. If the landing was successful, it could be every soul in England.

The song of the stones became almost dizzying, like a fingertip running around the rim of a brandy glass – high, resonant and piercing – a siren. And somewhere below the sound, somewhere far below the lantern room, there was another sound. A murmur of voices, and a little dry sound, rather like the cough of a fox.

It can't be . . .

Mrs Baron watched the hypnotic beam of light and, while she was facing away from me, I did the only thing that I *could* do. I hauled myself forward in the chair, stretching out as far as I possibly could, fingers reaching, reaching, until I caught the brass end of the speaking tube with my fingertips and brought it quickly to my mouth. I blew as hard as I could through the tube, praying that the whistle was fitted to the other end. Sure enough, the shrill sound echoed up from the kitchen. Mrs Baron spun around and strode towards me to swat the speaking tube from my hands. It clattered loudly to the floor.

'What are you doing, you stupid girl? Do you think that will stop me? There is no one at the other end. No one to help you. Your grandfather is in Dover. Your stupid sister is unconscious. Your father is dead. Your mother is locked up, miles and miles away from here.'

Her voice swelled with manic pride. 'I knew that she was innocent, of course, and I *am* sorry about what happened. But it was better to have her locked up than to risk losing the *real* collaborator – the one I needed – the one who was capable of passing on such useful information direct from the Admiralty.'

'Pa,' I breathed. 'You knew Pa was the spy?'

'Of course I knew it was him. *I made him do it.*'

What?

'When my contact in Germany asked for military maps of the coastline, activity of naval vessels, diagrams with coordinates of the local shipping hazards – the sandbank and so on – I knew that there was only one man around here in a position to provide them. And I knew he couldn't be bought by the Nazis at any price. So I started digging . . . I looked in the marriage register – and I struck gold straight away. No one attended your parents' wedding except two family members from your mother's side: her aunt and her cousin, Max. They were both witnesses for the marriage and so their full names are in the register. My contact in Berlin recognized the cousin's name straight away. He is in Hitler's Gestapo now – a very powerful man – and your stupid mother had been sending him birthday and Christmas cards right up until last year.'

The man with the little blond beard . . . So there had been another reason for hiding the wedding photograph, then. It could have been used as evidence against Mutti – evidence that she was in contact with a member of the Nazi secret police.

'This placed your family in a very vulnerable position indeed.' She chuckled oddly. 'I sent an anonymous letter to your father, demanding that he deliver the required information to our pick-up point, or your mother's contacts with Hitler's government would be exposed – to the police and to the press. Your father, I'm delighted to say, was very compliant.'

So Pa had been blackmailed. He had had no choice. Even when Pinstripe had given him the chance to tell the truth, he had refused, preferring to die a traitor than to endanger Mutti by revealing the truth about her cousin Max.

'And your mother even confessed! The perfect scapegoat, walking herself willingly to the slaughter – very obliging of her!'

'But the police know it wasn't her. That detective from London – he knows it was Pa. And soon they will know that *you* were the one behind it all.'

'*How* will they know, Petra? Who do you think is going to tell them?' As she spoke, the beam of light swept over the sea and I thought I saw something – a little shoal of shapes, dark against the shining water. Could those be the landing craft from the U-boat?

I have to shut the lamp off. I managed to shuffle forwards in my seat – just a little, and Mrs Baron turned to watch me struggle. 'This country is going to be magnificent,' she said, and her eyes gleamed. 'It will be a newer, cleaner world – ordered and perfect – exactly as my husband said it would be!' She pulled a small bottle from her pocket, opened it, and tipped some of the contents on to a white cloth. 'And nothing will stop us,' she hissed, taking a step towards me. 'I had no qualms about putting your sister to sleep when she tried to stand in my way, and I'm more than happy to dispatch you too, Petra. Obstacles along the path to glory must be removed!'

44

Planes roared across the sky as Mrs Baron pushed the white cloth into my face.

It smelt like strong alcohol, or something you'd use to clean a kitchen sink. I gulped in a quick breath of clean air and tried to duck out of the way, wriggling back in my chair, but then I heard something – footsteps on the lighthouse stairs, a shout. Mrs Baron twisted towards the noise and I shoved her hard with both hands. She fell heavily, dropping the cloth and the glass bottle which shattered on the floor.

'You're not going to stop me,' she screamed, scrabbling to get up, and I saw her reach for the heavy iron handle that cranks up the optic. 'You stupid little girl! You pathetic little mouse!' As she lurched towards me, raising the crank above her head, a figure plunged into the lantern room and hurled itself at her. It took just a moment for me to recognize my brilliant, heroic sister. Mags tackled the shrieking woman, trying to wrestle the crank handle from her. Mrs Baron caught her hard on the chin with it, but Mags wrapped herself around Mrs Baron's back and clung on like a limpet, stopping her from getting back on to her feet.

Light blasted around us and the sound of engines in the sky was almost deafening, but I wasn't afraid any more. I was full of fire now – this monster had taken so much from me already, I wasn't going to let her destroy me or my sister or our Castle. I launched myself out of the chair and landed heavily, driving all the breath from my body. Gasping, clawing, I hauled myself across the floor. I pushed myself up with one hand, and with the other I snatched at the lever of the lamp and shoved it upwards.

The darkness rushed back around us, thick as a swarm of bees.

There was a violent scraping noise, a thud and a cry of pain.

'Mags!'

Then footsteps down the staircase – quick and light.

Mrs Baron was getting away!

There were scuffling screams on the steps. Then a familiar voice: 'She got past me – I'm going after her.' It was Pinstripe! So I *had* heard his dry little cough.

'Sergeant! Get up there and help the girls,' he shouted. Within seconds, a young policeman appeared, wearing a muddy uniform and holding a torch. 'Can I help you, miss?' he said, bending over me.

'No,' I said, 'help Mags – help my sister.'

The beam of his torch picked out the lump that lay on the floor – perfectly still.

'Is she all right?'

'I think so,' he said. 'Unconscious, though. I'll take her down to the kitchen, then I'll come back for you.'

He was down the stairs with Mags in his arms and back again for me within a minute.

'Wait,' I said. 'There's something I need to do first.' I had been listening to the soft whirring of the optic. It was growing fainter and fainter . . . and then it stopped. Mrs Baron hadn't turned the handle for long enough.

I strained up from the floor one last time. I reached for the lever, and pulled it down hard.

Blinding light pierced the darkness, blasting out towards the sea in one fixed, steady beam.

'Miss!' the policeman exclaimed. 'You can't do that! The blackout! There are planes . . .'

'I know,' I said. 'But right now this is more important. There's a German U-boat out there in the Channel, and this is the signal for them to abandon the landing.'

'There's a *what*?!'

'You need to use the telephone in the service room downstairs, Sergeant – contact the Admiralty straight away.'

45

Down in the kitchen, the sergeant placed me carefully in the wheelchair I use when I'm in the cottage. I looked at the mud and chalk stains all over his uniform and wondered what on earth had happened to him on his way to the lighthouse. He got me a glass of water and put a blanket around me. 'For the shock,' he said. Mags was lying on the window seat, unconscious beneath another blanket.

'Is she all right – my sister?'

'She'll be just fine. Pulse like a lion's. She'll come round any minute, I'm sure.'

Then Pinstripe came into the kitchen with Mrs Baron, her wrists handcuffed together. 'Found her out on the cliff,' he said. 'Flashing her little torch at the sea.'

'I wasn't!' she shouted. 'I was trying to get away from these girls. They're insane! They had turned the lighthouse lamp on when there were planes about – German planes!' she panted. 'They must be mad – I was trying to stop them, but they attacked me! I'm the ARP warden, you know – I'm a *magistrate*!'

Pinstripe marshalled her into a chair. He cleared his throat – his familiar little fox-cough. 'I'm afraid it's no use, Mrs Baron. I heard you,' he said. 'I heard everything you said, through this.' And he held up the speaking tube. 'Just as well Petra had the presence of mind to alert us by sounding the whistle.'

Pinstripe whispered something to the muddy sergeant, who immediately disappeared through the kitchen door. Then he turned back to Mrs Baron shivering with rage in her chair. 'I heard you say that you have a contact in Germany, that you are responsible for passing on information to the enemy, that you blackmailed Petra's father into colluding in an act of treachery, and that you have, tonight, been attempting to help stage an enemy landing. You are, in short, a traitor. And we've also been able to connect you directly to the acts of sabotage carried out by your son earlier in the summer.'

'The sabotage? But how could you possibly—'

'We have his confession, Mrs Baron.'

Everything stopped then. Mrs Baron sat perfectly still and stared at the inspector, the bones of her shoulders rising and falling with each breath. 'His . . . What do you *mean*? Michael is dead.'

And then the kitchen door opened, and we all turned towards it.

It was a ghost. The ghost of Michael Baron.

His hair was long and greasy. He was as thin as a garden rake. His clothes were dirty, and there was a terrible stench as he limped into the kitchen. The sergeant followed behind him, one hand on the boy's filthy shoulder. I saw then that Michael's wrists were handcuffed in front of him.

Mrs Baron had not moved. Her red-rimmed eyes were staring at her son. 'Michael,' she breathed, attempting to get up, but Pinstripe pushed her gently back into her chair. 'Michael – you're supposed to be down at Dragon Bay with a lantern. What are you doing here?'

'Dragon Bay?' I said, incredulous. 'He's supposed to be *dead*, isn't he?'

'I'm sorry, Mother,' Michael whispered, and his once-handsome chin quivered pathetically. 'They found me. I've told them everything.'

'You've . . .'

'Yes.'

And then there was another voice. 'It's because of me,' said Mags from the window seat. She sat up, holding her head. 'It's all my fault.'

46

'I think perhaps you ought to give us a full explanation, Miss Smith.'

My sister looked at Pinstripe. 'Yes.' But she didn't address what followed to the detective, she looked at me instead. 'I joined the search for Michael after the bomb, just as I said I would, right after the ambulance took you away, Pet. I was the first person to find him. He was up on the clifftop in the middle of the gorse bushes – he must have been thrown backwards by the blast. His leg was broken. Michael begged me not to call for help. He said if I called the police, he would be arrested for sabotage. He told me that it was *you* who had cut the telephone line, Pet.'

'*Me?*'

My sister was embarrassed then. Worse than embar-

297

rassed – ashamed. 'Yes. And that he'd tried to stop you.'

'And you *believed* him?'

'No. Maybe for a while.'

Pinstripe looked at her unblinkingly. So did Mrs Baron. And so did I.

'Yes. I believed him.' She couldn't look at Michael. 'It was easier to believe that my innocent little sister had been manipulated by someone – got herself tangled up in something stupid – than to believe that—'

I finished the sentence for her. 'Than to believe that your boyfriend was a Nazi.'

Her eyes filled up with tears. 'Yes.'

'So you hid him.' And I knew where. I had seen the mud and the chalk on the policeman's uniform. 'In Dragon Bay Cave.'

Mags looked at me almost gratefully. 'Yes. Mrs Baron and I moved him there together. She agreed it was best for Michael not to come here – just in case the police believed Petra's "spiteful nonsense".'

I shot the Baron a look, and then turned back to Mags. 'And you've been taking him food from the lighthouse,' I continued, the riddle of my poor dwindled sister making sense at last. 'You've been sharing your rations with him. That's why you've got so thin, Mags.'

A tear ran down the side of my sister's face. 'I wanted so much to believe that he was innocent. He was very ill – I went to see him every day to look after him. But then, as he got stronger, he started telling me things – things that he thought about the world, about the war. He had persuaded me to take him out in the boat several times before the bomb. He had asked me about the sandbank, and the lighthouse, about the tides. I thought he was just showing an interest in boats because he liked me, but——'

Mrs Baron interrupted her then. 'But he was just using you for information. You were *useful*,' she sneered. 'Michael and I planned exactly how to get what we needed from you. You were so easy to manipulate. Just like your pathetic father.'

If my legs had worked, I'd have flown across the room and clawed her nasty red eyes out.

'As the weeks went by, it got harder and harder for me to believe that Michael had told me the truth,' Mags went on. She wiped both eyes with the back of her hand. 'Today I asked Petra if what she had said about Michael was true and she said——'

'I said I couldn't remember.'

Mags smiled through her tears then. 'Yes. But I'm your big sister, Pet. I can always tell when you're lying, remember? I knew you were trying to protect me from the truth. I went straight to Michael in the cave and confronted him. He told me everything, and he begged me to help him tonight – just one last thing, he said. I needed to help him get down to Dragon Bay, and then come back and light the lamp at exactly eleven o'clock.'

'But this time you refused.'

'I went straight to the police station and told them everything. I told them where to find Michael, and that he and his mother were planning something to do with the lighthouse and Dragon Bay. And then, when I got home, *she* was here.' She pointed at Mrs Baron. 'She told me what she wanted me to do and I refused. Then there was a struggle – I remember the little bottle in her hand and—'

'I should have finished you off,' Mrs Baron screeched. 'You nasty little—'

Then Michael spoke. He had been silent all this time, listening to Mags tell her story. 'I *do* love you, Magda,' he said. 'I didn't to begin with – you were just part of the plan. But I do love you now, I swear.' His mother's face grimaced, sickened. Michael shuffled towards my sister and opened his green eyes wide. I remembered the way they used to sparkle, but it wasn't like this – crazed, feverish. 'Starting the fires, cutting the telephone lines, telling you a few white lies along the way, even the fact that I had to threaten your sister that night – they were all necessary: just the means to an end. Sometimes you have to be ruthless.'

Mags suddenly locked her eyes upon him, and I saw that they were as cold as pebbles. 'You threatened my sister?' she whispered.

'Yes – and I'm sorry I had to do that, but anyone can see that sacrifices have to be made if people like you and me are to have the future we deserve. Anyone can see that *welcoming* the invasion is the quickest route to peace. The only right side in this war is the winning side.' He was even closer to her now. 'And I want you to be on that side with me, Mags. It's not too late. Our police – these idiots – they'll have no power at all when Hitler's army arrive – and they're on their way right now! I will look after you, I promise.' He reached out a filthy, handcuffed paw and took my sister's hand. He was looking steadily at her as he lifted her fingers towards his lips and kissed them.

I studied her face. I waited.

I knew what was coming, because I knew my sister, and I knew that look. 'I don't really need looking after, thank you, Michael, and even if I did, I don't think you'd be in a position to do so,' she said, pulling her hand away very gently, and then wiping it on her coat in disgust. 'After all, it's the death penalty for traitors.'

47

It was after midnight when Grandpa Joe got home. He came into the cottage, pale and exhausted, his white hair dripping with rain. As soon as the all-clear had been given, he had walked all the way back to us from Dover, through the cold and rain. I thought that it was the sort of magnificent thing my Pa would have done.

'I knew it!' he said, when we told him about everything that had happened. 'I knew that Baron woman was up to something. Months ago, I saw her out early in the morning, heading to the telephone box on the Dover Road. She made a habit of it, and I thought it was so odd, I even started writing it all down. Like the posters say — you know, report anything unusual or suspicious. But then a pair of monkeys turned up one morning . . .'

Mags and I looked at each other. I felt my cheeks redden as I remembered Mags scampering across the grass to steal Joe's scribbled note.

'The whole thing went clean out of my head after your Pa died . . .' And he shook his head, angry at himself. 'Why on earth did I trust her? Why did I leave you alone? You could have been killed last night, the pair of you.'

'We're all right, though, Grandpa Joe,' I said. And then I thought about what he'd just said. 'So the MB on that piece of paper was Mrs Baron – not Michael?'

'*Meredith* Baron,' he said. 'There was a picture of her in the local newspaper and I'd seen her in the village a few times.'

'Meredith?' I'd never thought of the Baron as someone who might possess a first name. 'And TB stood for telephone box!' I said triumphantly.

Grandpa Joe chuckled. 'You've cracked it, Pet.'

'Hardly a complicated code, though,' said Mags.

'I don't know,' I said. 'I could never make sense of the numbers.'

'What did they look like?'

'Four digits and then a gap and then six more.'

'Like this,' Grandpa Joe wrote a row of numbers on the back of the newspaper that sat on the kitchen table. He smiled gently at the puzzle:

0032 011140

'You should be able to get this, Pet. You help with the lighthouse logbook often enough.'

And suddenly it became clear.

'They're times, aren't they?' I said. I remembered that when Pa recorded the weather or shipping information in his logbook, he didn't write the time in words as 'twenty past six', or 'five o'clock', and he didn't use any dots or colons either; he wrote the time like this: 0620 or 0500. 'So the longer numbers are the date,' I said. 'I remember they all ended with 40. So 0032 011140 is—'

'Is well past your bedtime, ladies,' Grandpa Joe said, standing up. 'Now, are you sure we don't need to get you a doctor, Mags?'

'I'm fine,' she said, rubbing her head. 'Just a bump.'

Joe smiled at the two of us with his sad eyes that shone just like Pa's, and then he wheeled me through the passageway to the bedroom. 'Pair of troopers, you two,' he said quietly. 'Pair of blooming troopers.'

48

I tried to sleep, but all night long there were noises drifting up to the Castle from the bay below: voices and engines – blurred sounds amidst the shushing of the waves and the rain. Then, at last, silence. Pinstripe had said the military would be dealing with everything now. He had said not to worry. But I needed to know what those sounds meant.

Had any of the landing craft made it to the shore? Had our men got there in time?

It wasn't until the next morning that we found out what had happened. Mags ran down to the village at first light to ask Edie what she had heard, but she knew nothing about any of it, and nor did anyone else. She said she knew Kipper's fishing fleet had gone out as usual. In the end, Mags went to the police station and found Pinstripe.

It turned out that the planned landing was not the glorious invasion that Mrs Baron and Michael had anticipated: there were only three landing boats, and they had all turned back as soon as I had changed the signal from the lighthouse. The U-boat had melted away into the dark water.

'It's as if it never even happened,' I said to Pinstripe.

Mags had brought him back to the lighthouse with her. We sat together in the lantern room, and she brought us up a tray of tea and two buttered slices of fruitcake before disappearing back to the kitchen. I was glad she didn't stay. There were things I wanted to ask the detective that would have upset or embarrassed my sister, and perhaps she felt the same.

Pinstripe told me that he had had suspicions about Mrs Baron and her son for some time – he'd been sure they were linked to the acts of sabotage. It turned out that Mrs Baron's husband had been a member of the British Union of Fascists. He had even taken his family to one of Hitler's rallies in Germany. Mrs Baron moved away from London after his death, somehow managing to conceal her own political beliefs from the authorities. For the last year or so, she and Michael had been working to help prepare for the invasion. She had been taking orders from a friend of her husband in Berlin – sending him packages of information and coded messages via a secret collection point – the telephone box on the Dover Road.

'The piece of paper you left at the police station gave us an important breakthrough,' Pinstripe said. 'The one you left with the constable on the night you reported Michael Baron.' He settled himself into the wicker chair with his cup of tea and smiled at me. 'An excellent bit of detective work there.'

'It wasn't me,' I said. 'It was Grandpa Joe.'

'Ah.' Pinstripe took the scrap of paper from his pocket. 'Well, it was vital evidence. We knew when and where the packages were arriving in London, so as soon as we received this list, we knew Mrs Baron had been at the drop-off point on exactly those days.'

I looked at the scrap of paper, amazed that it had turned out to be useful after all. 'I didn't think the policeman was going to give it to you,' I said, remembering the sneer on Oily's face as he suggested that I was just a spiteful little girl.

'He didn't at first,' Pinstripe admitted. 'But when I arrived at the police station later that evening, he told me that the scruffy child from the lighthouse had been in with some tall tale about the magistrate's son, and that she had had the cheek to bother him with this *bit of scribbled nonsense*.'

I blushed at the bit about being scruffy.

'I knew what it meant as soon as I saw it,' he went on. 'Mrs Baron went very quiet after Michael went missing, though. The deliveries to London seemed to stop altogether, so there was no chance of catching her red-handed. And you won't believe the trouble I had trying to get a warrant to search a magistrate's house. It was only after your sister came to the police station yesterday and Michael was arrested that we were finally granted permission to search the property.

'We found some papers belonging to her late husband; a Nazi flag, which they were intending on flying from their window in the event of an invasion; a radio, and a set of instructions for signalling to the U-boat. That note had yesterday's date on it. When I saw that the lighthouse was indeed part of her plan, I came up to the Castle straight away. And the rest you know, Petra.'

'Yes.' The rest I knew.

I watched a young seagull launching into the air, gliding all the way down from the top of the light-house, over the raw edge of the cliff.

It had been hard to get used to that new gap on the clifftop where the bomb had fallen. It reminded me of the jagged tear across the middle of our family tree – Pa and Mutti ripped away from us, just the daughters left behind, so close to the edge . . .

'Do you think they will ever let Mutti come home?' I said.

'At some point. Provided the authorities believe she is no threat to security. It seems that her cousin in the

Gestapo was killed by resistance fighters in France last month.'

I took in a little sharp breath. 'You knew about him?'

'Yes.' He nodded. 'And I know that your mother's communication with him was entirely innocent. It seemed that she was still fond of the little boy she remembered from childhood; she had no idea about the sort of man he had become. It would really be something if her annual Christmas card message of *Frohe Weihnachten!* turned out to be some kind of complex code.' The lines of his face folded into a smile. 'Your mother was convinced that Magda was in trouble – did you know that? She had asked her where she was going so early in the mornings and Magda had lied to her – said she was working on the motor boat at the harbour.'

'She didn't want us to know about Michael.'

'No.'

It was all making sense now. 'Mutti suspected Mags had got involved with something bad, didn't she? That was why she wanted us both to be evacuated.'

'Yes.'

'And that was why she confessed to being a spy. She had no idea it was Pa who'd actually sent the documents – she assumed it must be Mags. She was trying to protect her.'

'That's right.'

I thought back to Mutti's letter — *Remember that I have told the policeman everything he needs to know. I am ready now to tell them that it was me, to write it down and sign it. I'm so sorry, my darlings. This is the best way. I love you all so much.* This had been her coded message to Mags. Her way of telling her daughter that she was taking the blame, and warning her to keep quiet.

'Mutti was right in a way, though, wasn't she?' I said. 'Mags was helping the Barons to prepare for the enemy landing — although she didn't really know it.'

'It's her naivety that has saved your sister from prosecution,' he said. 'Sadly, your father made a conscious decision — he gave in to Mrs Baron's blackmail in an attempt to protect your mother.'

'I haven't told the others,' I said then. 'I haven't told anyone what Pa did.'

Pinstripe looked at me strangely. 'How did you know about it, Petra? How did you know that he was responsible for sending the documents?'

I nodded towards the speaking tube. 'I found out about Pa in the same way that you heard Mrs Baron's confession — through the speaking tube,' I said. 'The day before Dunkirk. I heard Pa tell you the truth.'

Pinstripe smiled a little. 'Well, there's no reason for anyone to know now,' he said slowly. 'They'll find out soon enough what Mrs Baron did. They'll know that your sister was manipulated by Michael Baron, and that your mother is completely innocent. Let them remember your father as the man who saved the lives of many, many people – with his lighthouse and his lifeboat.' He looked straight at me and crinkled his craggy brow. 'But that's a very heavy secret to carry around all by yourself, Petra.'

'Yes,' I said. 'But I'm strong enough to carry it.'

We sat quietly for a while, watching the steady roll of the whale-grey waves. The U-boat had gone, but its cold, threatening presence somehow remained – lurking there in the murky water, just like the Wyrm. *But, for now, there will be no more sacrifices,* I thought. *For now, those monstrous, writhing shadows will have to stay hungry.*

I often think about the song I sang when I was sitting up on the cliffs, waiting for Pa and Mags to return from Dunkirk. In the smoky light of that dawn, a spell was woven that would bind me to the magic of the clifftops and the stones for ever. The doctor says that the feeling in my legs could come back any day, or it may never come back at all. I try not to think about it. Instead, I think about how proud I am.

I know that I am part of a story that is thousands of years old. In years to come, people will whisper the tale to their children – a tale about love and loyalty: the legend of the Last Daughter of Stone.

It is about a girl who was small and unnoticeable and frightened. A girl whose mother was locked away and whose father was lost at sea. A child who battled with monsters, braving the raging skies and the darkness of the night to protect her castle: Defender of the White Cliffs. Dragon Slayer. Daughter of Stone.

Now, when I write the name Petra Zimmermann Smith, it no longer feels several sizes too big for me. I find it is a name that fits me perfectly.

EPILOGUE

Spring 1941

They are not interested in us any more. The enemy planes keep high, soaring above us here on the coast and heading inland instead. Yesterday, Grandpa Joe said that Hitler now seems to be less concerned with invading us, and more interested in bombing London into submission. It is very strange hearing the roar of the engines, and knowing that someone's home is about to be destroyed – a shop, a pub, a whole street, reduced to smoke and rubble.

It is very nearly a year now since Dunkirk. Nearly a year since we lost Pa. I think about him every day, especially when I am alone up in the lantern room. Sometimes I talk to him, telling him all our news. I told him when Mutti was moved to a new internment camp on the Isle of Man – a nicer place, full of artists and musicians. I tell him the gossip from the village, or that Grandpa Joe is well and enjoying being a lighthouse keeper once more, or about how plump and bright-eyed Mags is these days. Sometimes I just listen to the warm echoes of Pa's voice in my mind, as he tells me stories about shipwrecks and smugglers, mermaids and dragons. Sometimes – just for a second – I allow myself to believe that the tuneless whistling coming from the service room isn't Grandpa Joe at all – it is actually Pa: he's just downstairs, and he'll come up to see me in a minute, and salute me in that silly way of his and call me First Mate. But I don't let myself imagine that very often, because it makes the sea and the sky go all blurry, and my throat starts to hurt, and the pages of my sketchbook get spoilt with salt-water splodges.

It is a glorious spring day today, and Grandpa Joe and I are the only ones at home. Mags has gone into Dover with Kipper Briggs. They have been stepping out together for a couple of months now. He holds his head up high these days and I swear he looks handsome in a way that he never did before. *Kipper the Skipper*. It's funny really – there was something terrible inside Michael Baron that we did not know was there, and there was something wonderful inside Kipper. He and Mags spend every Sunday together, working on his fleet of fishing boats. Not my idea of romance, but I've never seen Mags look so strong and happy. She has stopped using hats and hair-dos to disguise her sticking-out ears, and she has *Essential Motor Boat Maintenance* on permanent loan from the library.

Grandpa Joe has asked Mags to pick up a copy of *The Times* while she's in Dover ('because you get a much better shine when you polish the lantern with a good quality newspaper'), and a part we need to repair a worn-out section of the optic mechanism. He says the lighthouse is a beacon of hope and, when the war is over, the lamp will shine all the time, so we need to look after it properly. I am looking forward to the light very much, but I find I am now much less afraid of the darkness.

I am sitting up here in the lantern room, as usual, with Barnaby curled up beside me like an enormous purring cushion. Grandpa Joe is making lunch downstairs in the kitchen. He is singing a sea shanty: 'I'll come home to my darling one, home to my love . . .'

I listen, and gaze out into the bright morning. My sketchbook is on my lap, my pencil in my hand. *There is a peculiar quality to the light today*, I think. The sea shimmers strangely, as if it is merely an illusion – a mirror of the blue sky above. The Wyrm lies quiet – deeply asleep. There is no breeze. No sea birds are calling, and there are no boats humming through the water or planes rumbling above. I think I can hear a high, fine thread of song – is it coming from the stones on the clifftop, or is it inside me? It seems to shimmer: it is taut, expectant, magical.

I manage to shift my chair around a little to face inland. I want to draw a different view today.

I draw the overlapping folds of the fields, and the spire of Stonegate church. And then I draw a dot on the distant Dover Road. The dot becomes a car. I start to draw more quickly – sketching one image after another: the car has taken the track between the pea field and the cabbage field and is stopping by the gate at the end of our garden . . . I realize I am holding my breath. I flip the page of my sketchbook.

I draw a lady climbing out of the rear door of the car. For the first time since the accident, I feel blood rushing into my legs; my whole body is straining to move, to leap up and fly down the stairs towards her, to run down the path and into her arms. But I know that I can't do that – I must stay here and wait. It isn't real yet. I must draw it first.

The lady looks very thin and tired. She is clutching a handkerchief in her fist – she has been crying, and, as she stands there, looking up at the Castle, she begins to cry once more. She holds on to the fence to steady herself.

An old man has walked down the path from the cottage to the garden gate. I draw him holding the gate open for the lady to come through. The two of them stand there for a moment, neither of them saying anything. The old man holds out his hand, then it falls back to his side again. It is a strange gesture – he does not know what to do, and she does not know what to do either. Then he opens both his arms and she steps quickly into his embrace.

I draw them standing together, her face pressed against his shoulder. She is crying, and there are tears running down his face too. He pats her back gently, as a father would his child. Perhaps he is saying something to her very quietly. Perhaps she understands.

I draw them walking up the path to the cottage, side by side. He carries her suitcase for her. She is looking up towards me here in the lantern room. The hand clutching the handkerchief is over her heart, and I wonder if hers is aching as much as mine is at this moment.

Do you think she can see me up here? The bright sun is behind me. I am just a shadow at the moment.

The song of the stones is humming soft and sweet all around the lighthouse now.

Today is the day, I think, *for one last miracle*.

I lift my hand from the paper at last, and dare to look out of the window.

HISTORICAL NOTE

Our Castle by the Sea is mostly set during the first year of the Second World War. While the story of Petra and her family is entirely fictional, the events happening around them – such as the formation of the Local Defence Volunteers and the passing of the Treachery Act in May 1940 – are very real indeed.

'Enemy aliens' (German, Austrian and Italian nationals living in Great Britain) were assessed and categorized at tribunals, and many thousands were interned. A significant percentage of these were refugees, but the situation was seen to be urgent and dangerous: the risk of foreign spies helping the enemy threatened Britain's war effort. It was considered too complicated and time-consuming to separate those who were fleeing the Nazis from those who supported them, so they were all interned together.

Thousands of foreign nationals were deported. The SS *Arandora Star* was hit by torpedoes from a German U-boat on 2 July 1940. Over 800 people died, most of whom were male German and Italian internees being deported to Canada together with some German prisoners of war.

German U-boats were active in the Channel during the latter months of 1939, but not – as far as I know – in October 1940, and there was no attempted landing on the Kent coast at this time, so this is perhaps the point at which I have taken the greatest liberties with the truth for the purposes of Petra's story.

The story is set on the coast of Kent, not far from Dover, but Dragon Bay and the village of Stonegate are fictional. Petra's 'Castle' is inspired partly by both the North Foreland and South Foreland lighthouses, and Goodwin Sands sparked the idea of the dreaded Wyrm.

Following Germany's invasion of France on 10 May 1940, British, Belgian and French forces were trapped along the north coast of France. Between 26 May and 4 June, over 300,000 Allied soldiers were evacuated from the beaches and harbour of Dunkirk. Hundreds of British fishing boats, lifeboats and pleasure craft assisted in the evacuation. The situation for the Allies had looked hopeless, and the successful rescue of so many men was described by the British Prime Minister Winston Churchill as a 'miracle'.

ACKNOWLEDGEMENTS

The writing of *Our Castle by the Sea* was a project supported by Arts Council England, so I would like to begin by thanking this wonderful institution for all the utterly brilliant work they do.

Thank *you*, the reader, for meeting me halfway with your extraordinary imagination, for enjoying my story, for becoming attached to my characters, and for getting in touch to tell me all about your favourite bits. Thank you to all the bookworms, book bloggers, teachers, librarians, reviewers and Twitterers out there for loving children's literature and telling the world that it is important.

Enormous thanks, as always, to the one and only Barry Cunningham and to Rachel Leyshon – the kindest and cleverest editor in the business: no one else can light the blue touchpaper (creatively speaking) quite like Rachel does. Thank you also to all the fabulous Chickens – Rachel H, Laura, Jazz, Elinor, Kesia, Sarah, Esther and Lucy – for your continued enthusiasm, hard work and diligence, and for your patience when I was trying to edit the book at the same time as being heavily pregnant/looking after a new baby! I love being part of the Chicken House coop, and am so grateful for the support of all my fellow Chicken authors – you guys rock the reading world.

Thank you to Daphne (the genius copy-editor), my

meticulous proofreader, and to my friend and historical consultant Graham Noble for giving me so much of his precious time: please accept my humble apologies for the points at which I have chosen the integrity of the story over factual precision. Helen Crawford-White has, as always, worked her unique magic with the cover design and illustrations – thank you, Helen, for this beautiful interpretation of Petra and her clifftop home.

Thank you to Luigi and Alison Bonomi for offering not only representation and creative advice, but kindness and friendship as well. I am so happy and grateful to be tucked beneath the LBA wing.

Thanks also go to Kinn Hamilton Mcintosh and Heather Stennett for all their painstaking work in this corner of Kent, gathering local accounts of the Second World War. Their collections of real memories from the war were so valuable to me in creating this story.

My friends and colleagues at Kent College Canterbury have been the most fantastic help facilitating and encouraging my work as a writer. Particular thanks go to the English Department for cheering me on, and for stepping in as proofreaders at the last minute!

Many thanks to the hard-working and knowledgeable volunteers at the many lighthouses I visited during my research, particularly those at the South Foreland Lighthouse at St Margaret's Bay. Thanks also to the staff at the beautiful Belle Tout Lighthouse, Beachy Head. I must mention here the paintings of Eric Ravilious which I love so much, especially the view from the Belle Tout lantern room which was the starting point for this book.

I am profoundly grateful for the support of my lovely friends, my amazing parents, all the Strange clan and the Barbers too! A special thank you to my wonderful partner James, who has driven me to lots of lighthouses and kept me smiling through what has been the most incredible year of challenges and miracles. Thank you for your help with this book and for your hugs and encouragement when it was all a bit overwhelming.

Thank you to the Moo for dozing by my side during those long and difficult rewrites, and, last but by no means least, thank you little Fred (aka Grumbledore) – even though you won't be able to read this for a few years yet – for making me the happiest mum in the world. I have so many wonderful stories to tell you, my darling.

ALSO BY LUCY STRANGE

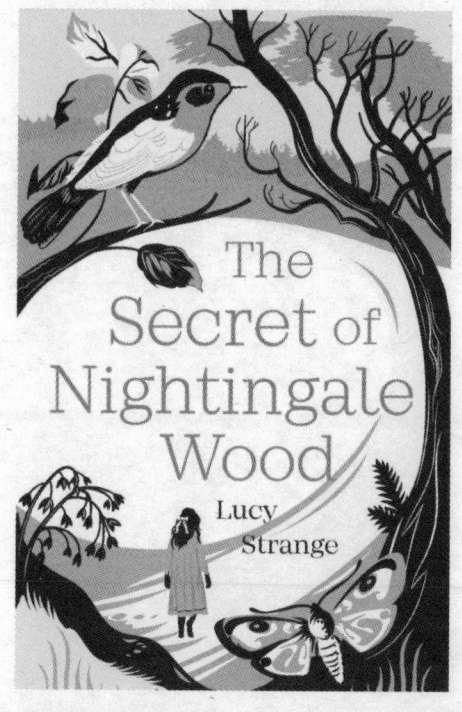

THE SECRET OF NIGHTINGALE WOOD

Something terrible has happened in the Abbott family and nobody is talking about it.

Mama is ill. Father has taken a job abroad. Nanny Jane is too busy looking after baby Piglet to pay any attention to Henrietta and the things she sees – or thinks she sees – in the shadows of their new home, Hope House.

All alone, with only stories for company, Henry discovers that Hope House is full of strange secrets: a forgotten attic, thick with cobwebs; ghostly figures glimpsed through dusty windows; mysterious firelight that flickers in the trees beyond the garden.

One night she ventures into the darkness of Nightingale Wood. What she finds there will change her whole world . . .

Paperback, ISBN 978-1-910655-03-0, £6.99 • ebook, ISBN 978-1-910655-63-4, £6.99